MAMA'S PLACE

MAMA'S PLACE

A Redneck Chronicle

Jim Feazell

iUniverse, Inc.
New York Bloomington

MAMA'S PLACE

iUniverse books may be ordered through booksellers or by contacting:

iUniverse
1663 Liberty Drive
Bloomington, IN 47403
www.iuniverse.com
1-800-Authors (1-800-288-4677)

ISBN: 978-1-4401-8906-7 (sc)
ISBN: 978-1-4401-8907-4 (ebook)

Printed in the United States of America

iUniverse rev. date: 10/29/2009

FOR ALL MY
REDNECK FRIENDS

PREFACE

Three years before the new state highway 7 opened between El Dorado and Camden—Mama's Place carried on a landslide business just barely outside the corporate limits on the south side of Smackover. Probably more beer was sold and consumed there than in any other such place in southern Arkansas. And there were a lot of them. Mama's Place was a large old degraded country home that nestled back from the highway behind a huge oak tree with plenty of space for parking. On top of the veranda roof, a large red on white sign, lighted by a spotlight, brightly designated it as being Mama's Place. Across the veranda, atop the door, a small red sign simply stated "entrance". Another door to the left had been removed and the space permanently boarded up, as had the windows. Outside lights that lit the veranda, the parking space and the big sign were turned off when Mama closed for the night. The inside had undergone extensive remodeling. The walls between the two front rooms and hallway had been removed making it one long room across the entire front of the house. The north end was made into a dance floor, with new flooring and a jukebox in the corner with nothing but country music. On the west side of the dance floor a new restroom was added, taking space from an interior bedroom where Mama slept.

Mama's Place, being on the edge of the city limits received city water and sewerage. In the south end of the long room were tables and chairs. Along the interior wall was a long bar with bar stools. The bar ran from the interior door, which had a sign over it "Private-Do Not Enter", almost to the dance floor. Behind the bar close to the door was a four foot long by two feet high hole cut through the wall with a counter top built into it for passing food orders through. Inside, through the door, what use to be the homes dinning room was now a storage room with cases upon cases of Coors and Budweiser beer and a large cooler. In the kitchen, Mama had a large grill put in with a vented hood. The back bedroom belonged to Mama's two daughters, Angie and Effie. One other major, but very necessary, improvement was the installation of central air and heat which was vented through the ceiling to every room in the house. Two vents were put in the long front room. The unit sat on the north side of the house behind Mama's garage which housed her nineteen sixty Cadillac Fleetwood Limousine.

About ten feet from the back of the house was an old sixty-foot two bedroom trailer house used by two young women, Agnes and Arlene, both in their mid-twenties with plain homely appearances and large breasts. They worked for Mama doing the cooking and waiting tables. Occasionally, if the money was right Mama required them to prostitute themselves. Which they did not mind at all. About another fifty yards back was a large storage building with sheds built around it that housed an old Case tractor and farming implements. At the north end of the storage building was another, same such, trailer house that Mama's sons, Tommy Ray and Arlo, lived in.

Entering Mama's Place for the first time one might have either one of two impressions. A roadside honkytonk or a sleazy beer joint. Mama however, did serve food, even though it was only hamburgers and country fries.

Biography:

Maurine Muldune, who became known only as Mama, was of medium height and just a tad more than pleasingly plump, with long naturally blonde hair, usually rolled up like a birds nest atop her head. She wore very little make-up, was fun loving and always ready with a coarse joke. She cursed excessively within an air of modest and friendly demure.

Maurine was born and raised in the very house that became Mama's Place. She attended high school in El Dorado where she was always queen of the walk. A beautiful young lady, she excelled in sports and drama and was liked by all. After graduating high school, giving no thought to college, she took a job at the local Dairy Queen where she worked until she lost her parents in an unavoidable automobile accident. Maurine being an only child, found herself alone with a sizable amount of money from an insurance policy left by her parents. After a time of mourning, being the fun loving person that she was, she began to party. She partied and partied and partied and continued to party. Maurine, being a very passionate girl, could not control her feverish desire for sex. During her years of partying, she gave birth to four children. A deaf and dumb daughter whom she named Angie, only because she liked the name. Two sons, Tommy Ray and Arlo, born a year apart, and another daughter whom she called Effie, after her own mother. If Maurine knew who the fathers were, she never said. Having put on another forty or so pounds and kids to raise, she decided to remodel the house and open a restaurant. Everyone close to Maurine deferred to her wishes and judgment without question. Those who knew her well, apperceived that the restaurant, was destined to become a redneck beer joint.

The term "redneck" originated from the red sunburned necks of farmers that worked all day in the fields. Somewhere along the way it was changed to designate scummy low-life poor white trash. But then along about the mid-sixties it had miraculously taken on a different terminology. That of a cultured intellectual and philosophical erudite. So then, to be referred to as a "redneck" was truly a compliment. Or so said Mama.

By early summer 1971, where this story begun, Mama's Place had thrived with local honkytonking rednecks since opening in the spring of 1967. Mama's kids were now 23, 19, 18, and 16 respectively. Mama had recently turned 40 without telling a soul. She had subjectively decided to remain 39 for the rest of her life. They had not seen Angie for four years. Shortly after opening the business, Angie told Mama in her unique way of communicating with her, that she was leaving.

This book is a work of FICTION:

The crude, abusive, smutty, obscene, filthy, vulgar and downright sinful language is solely the responsibility of the writer, and for the sake of reality, is absolutely intended.

CHAPTER 1

Sheriff Avery Munson, stepped into the boat, walked to the front, stepping over the other seats, and sit on the front seat with his shotgun across his lap. The Sheriff was short, plump, balding and wore horn rimmed glasses. He showed all of his forty-three years and exhibited an air of serious demeanor.

"Let's go, Billy." he said. "What the fuck are you waiting on?"

Billy Bob Henry, the Sheriffs young twenty year old Deputy stepped into the boat and pushed off with a paddle before sitting down. He begin to paddle out through the brush and overhanging tree branches. They were in a large marshy slough north of Smackover alongside the old Tucker road. There had been numerous re-

1

ports, one of which was somewhat reliable, of a Bigfoot creature crossing the road in this vicinity. The slough was the eastern most end of a huge and mysteriously feared swamp which bordered the northern perimeter of the town of Heaven some ten miles west of Smackover. Bigfoot creatures had increased in sightings since one was legitimately seen seventy miles west near Fouke. It seemed, since then, every place across the southern section of the state with a wooded area, swamp or slough wanted their own Bigfoot. Billy Bob paddled slowly toward some overhanging cypress branches when suddenly a big water moccasin hanging from a limb directly in front of them began to sway to and fro with it's head reared up and hissing at the oncoming boat.

"Goddamn-it-to-hell !" the Sheriff screamed as he scampered to the back of the boat. "Back up, Billy Bob!! Back up!! Back the fuck up!!" Billy Bob back paddled as fast as he could with the Sheriff leaned over clutched to his shoulder. In his attempt to get to the back of the boat he lost his new Sheriff's hat over the side. "Damn-it Sheriff, git off of me so's I can paddle." yelled Billy Bob. Back to their starting point at the road, the Sheriff stood up almost falling out of the boat. He sit down on the next seat looking scared and hateful at Billy Bob.

"Do you want to go back and git yer hat?" asked Billy Bob.

"Hell naugh. You tryin' ta'be some kind'a smart ass."

"But it's brand new Sheriff. You just bought it two weeks ago."

"I don't give a rat's ass. I'm not goin' back out there."

They got out of the boat and pulled it up on the road behind the trailer.

"Sheriff, why didn't you shoot that damn snake?" ask Billy Bob.

The Sheriff looked dumbfounded at Billy Bob for a few seconds before answering. "I didn't bring the God-damn shotgun out here to shoot snakes." he stammered. "I brought it to shoot a cock-suckin' Bigfoot. Let's load the fuckin' boat an' go home."

"Sheriff, you're bout as full of shit as a Christmas turkey, ya'know."

"That may be, boy, but I'm the Sheriff, you're just a little pip-squeak fart. So watch the fuck how you talk to me."

They loaded the boat and headed back to the Sheriff's office. Billy Bob Henry, was a handsome young man. He maintained a neat and well groomed appearance, always with combed hair, creased trousers and shined shoes. He had dark black hair and deep blue piercing eyes. That, along with a kindly smile, always gave him an advantage of predominate superiority in most any given situation.

The Sheriff, peeling an apple, sat leaned back in a wooden swivel chair behind his desk when Billy Bob returned from taking the boat and trailer to the garage. The Sheriff looked over his glasses at him. "Ya'know you come damn close ta'gittin' me snake bit out there today."

"Naugh, you come damn close ta'gittin' yerself snake bit. Ya'should of shot it."

"Listen you sorry little cunt. If you weren't the Mayor's nephew. I'd of fired yer worthless ass a long time ago."

"Like I'd really give a shit." Billy Bob laughed. "I ought to just git yer ass fired and take over yer job."

The Sheriff cut the peeled apple in half and cored each half. He laid it on his desk, wiped his red sweaty face and bald head. He looked questioningly at Billy Bob. "Are you gona be goin' out to Mama's Place ta'see that girl what yer so sweet on. What's her name—Effie?"

"Yeah, Effie. I reckon I will—why?"

"I want'cha ta'do a little undercover investigatin' fer us. You know, like fuckin' secret covert work."

"What'th hell you talkin' bout, Avery?"

"Ya'know." he said harshly. "I told'ya ta'always call me Sheriff. Where the fuck you git this Avery crap from?"

"Sorry, Sheriff. Didn't mean ta'ruffle yer feathers. I just forgot."

"That's why you'd never make a Sheriff. You have ta'be able ta'remember things. Now—what the fuck were we talkin' bout?"

"Something bout covert operations at Mama's Place."

"Oh yeah, do you remember Mama's oldest girl—Angie?"

"I never saw her. But I've heard all about'er."

"Okay, I want you ta'keep yer eyes and ears open. I have reason ta'think she might be livin' out in them woods somewhere."

"Av—Sheriff. She's been gone fer bout four years accordin'ta Effie."

"Yeah, I know that story. Mama said she got tired of all'th ridicule an' just took off." He picked up half of the apple, looked at it, and laid it down.

"Yeah, bout four or five years ago. Effie said all them people were working on the house and they always made fun of'er and picked on'er cause she was deaf and dumb. What makes'ya think she's out in them woods?"

"One of the women what works fer Mama told me she has seen Mama put out food, and clothin' an' stuff on Saturday nights after closing up. By early on Sunday morning it was always gone."

"Strange huh." said Billy Bob.

"Not to strange if'ya put the pieces together. I think she might be stayin' back in there at her brothers still."

"Holy mackerel!" Billy Bob exclaimed quite loudly. "Are'ya sayin' Tommy Ray and Arlo have a still.—A whiskey still."

"That's what I'm thinking. Hell they must have. You know that field below the house what was full of corn. I'd say bout five acres. Maybe six. I've never seen'em sell any of it, and it's all been picked. They don't have any stock ta'feed. What else do'ya reckon spring time sweet corn is used for."

"What?" asked Billy Bob.

"Shit fire, boy. It's used fer makin' corn liquor. Good ol', burn yer fuckin' guts out, moonshine whiskey. Now I don't want'ya to go down there like some damn nitwit comic book detective and give yerself away. Just be friendly and keep yer fuckin'eyes open. If'ya see anything spicious, just report it back ta'me. Think ya'might can handle that?"

"Avery, damn it man. Like I said afore. You're bout as full of shit as a Christmas turkey. Don't you spect that if Angie was stayin' at the still, if there really is one, that her brothers would see to her needs instead of Mama puttin' things outside fer her ta'pick up. If she is with them. Don't ya'think Mama would know it."

The Sheriff looked hatefully at Billy Bob and wiped his red sweaty face and bald head again as Billy Bob pointed at the apple. "You not gona really eat that shit are'ya?" The apple had turned dark brown from the exposure to the heat in the office. The Sheriff picked up the apple and threw it in the waste basket.

"Sheriff, why don't you git the air conditioner fixed before you have a heat stroke. I'm gittin' out of here. I'll keep my eyes open fer anything funny goin' on. What does Angie look like, I've heard that she is real pretty."

"Yeah, well pretty ain't the word fer it. She's downright damn good lookin'. Kinda' little with long black shinny hair, green eyes and is built like a brick shithouse. Yeah, she's something to see alright. When she smiles at'ya with those big green eyes sparkling. It makes a man damn near have'a fuckin' heart attack. Yeah, she's something ta'see alright. Kinda like that sweetie of yourn." The Sheriff wiped his face and head again. "Yeah boy, you sure know how ta'pick'em. You knockin' the bottom out of that yet?"

"No, not yet." Billy Bob grinned. "I've just been courting"

"Hell, you probably couldn't reach the bottom anyway. You'd have ta'be hung like me ta'do that."

"Ha! dream on!" Billy Bob exclaimed loudly as he walked out the door.

CHAPTER 2

Billy Bob took a bite of his hamburger as Mama came over and sit down at the table with him. She, in the last few years, had gradually put on more weight. Not to the point of being obese, but certainly enough to be referred to as fat. For Mama, jolly would be a more delicate description. She had a pretty girlish face with a double chin, not to mention pronounced love handles that stretched her exceedingly tight dresses. "I spoze you came ta'see Effie?" she asked.

"Yes mam." he answered. "Is she here?"

"She's out back helping her brothers build something. Billy Bob, you do know Effie is only sixteen years old?"

"Yes, mam."

"You've been comin' by ta'see her real often and well, I feel like it's my motherly duty ta'ask exactly what yer intentions are."

Billy Bob had taken a big bite of his hamburger and welcomed the time to think of an appropriate answer while he chewed.—"Mama mam, I admire and appreciate your forethought to protect your daughter and I want'cha to know that her virtues are perfectively safe with me. I like Effie very much and would like ta'spend more time with her to git'ta know'er better. And yes, let'er git to know me better too. And like I said mam, you can rest assured she will be safe with me. My intentions are honorable. I could not bring myself ta'disrespect her innocence or respectability. I came to ask you if I might have your permission ta'take her out to dinner and to a movie tonight. If'n see wants ta'go with me."

As Mama listened to him she was impressed by his politeness and manners. She could never remember seeing a customer remove his hat at a table in her place. Regardful of his proficient disposition, Mama's conniving mind harbored an ulterior motive for wanting Billy Bob to become sweet on Effie.

"Alright Billy Bob, then you've got my permission ta'take her to dinner and a movie. Long as you don't go tryin'ta git inta' her pants."

"Yes mam,—I mean no mam. No, I want be doin' that." Mama got up and went to the bar as Billy Bob got up, picked up his hat from the floor beside the chair, and put it on. He took out his wallet.

"The burger is on the house, Billy Bob. You'll find Effie around back."

"Thank you, mam."

Billy Bob, with butterflies in his stomach, went around the Place and walked back toward the storage house, he saw Effie and Tommy Ray nailing boards on the side of a new shed. It was the first time he had seen Effie in tight jeans, *she looks even more delectable than in dresses.* hc thought. Effie looked up and saw him. She dropped her hammer and ran to meet him. Tommy Ray came out a little way toward them, turned back toward the storage house and jokingly yelled. "Git yer guns men. It's a raid!!" Arlo, with his shotgun in hand, and their good friend, Freeman Blankenship excitedly ran out from around the storage house. Tommy Ray, nineteen, with scraggly brown hair and brown eyes was lanky with a nervous mannerism. He was considered to be the leader over Arlo and Freeman. Arlo, eighteen, brown hair and brown eyes, medium build and the least intelligent of the brothers, succumbed somewhat reluctantly to his brothers wishes. It was quite obvious to anyone that they had the same father. "What's happening T.R., what's goin' on!!" yelled Arlo.

"Hell, it's just Billy Bob." Freeman said. "He ain't no raid. Anyway Effie's done got'em tied up." Freeman Blanlenship, a big strapping young man, also nineteen, red hair and friendly, was a lifelong friend of Tommy Ray and Arlo. He was always with them and helping with their endevors.

"What th'fuck you doin' here Billy Bob?" asked Tommy Ray. They had always been friends up to the point of Billy Bob becoming a Deputy Sheriff. After which time they harbored a strong resentment for him due to their extreme dislike for the law.

"Turn my sister loose!" yelled Arlo, pointing his shotgun toward them.

"Hell, Arlo." Freeman said. "He ain't holdin' her. She's holdin' him."

"I came ta'see bout gittin' permission ta'take Effie ta'the picture show."

"I can tell'ya right off." said Tommy Ray. "The answer is not no. But hell no."

"Now, turn my sister loose!" demanded Arlo.

"Put that damn gun down, Arlo!" shouted Tommy Ray.

"Tommy Ray." Billy Bob said. "I already have permission from Mama." Tommy Ray glared at Billy Bob for a minute, dropped his hammer and stammered as he headed for the house. "Yall stay here, I'll see bout this shit." He then broke into a run for the house. Effie stretched to her tiptoes and gave Billy Bob a peck on his face. "You don't be kissin' my sister. Ya'hear me, Billy Bob!" yelled Arlo.

"Hey, Billy Bob." Freeman asked. "Do'ya know what's playin' at the Rialto down in El Dorado?"

"Yeah, it's Planet Of The Apes, with Charlton Heston."

"That's already on? Man, I sure want ta'see it. It spoze ta'be real good."

"Shut up Freeman." Arlo said. "Don't be talkin' ta'em."

Tommy Ray returned like a pup with it's tail tucked between it's legs.

"Effie, do'ya really want ta'go with'em?" asked Tommy Ray.

"Yes, I sure do." said Effie.

"T.R., whyn't we just shoot his ass right now." Arlo said. "Ya'know he's just gona be tryin' ta'fuck'er."

"Shut up, Arlo. You and Freeman go see what'ya can do bout gittin' some God-damn hat racks fer the restaurant."

As Billy Bob and Effie, arm in arm, started back toward the house, He noticed that Tommy Ray's old red pick-up truck over by the trailer was loaded with freshly picked corn. The shucks were brown from the early summer sun. "Effie." he said as they rounded the house. "I'm goin' home and clean up and change clothes. I don't want people ta'think I'm arrestin'ya."

"Bet you'd like to though, wouldn't you." she teased.

"Oh yeah.—Now hush that up. I'll pick'ya up bout five."

"Okay, Lawman." she gave him a swift kiss on the mouth and ran up the steps and into the front door of Mama's Place. Effie, petite, lovely and shapely, had long blonde hair like her mother, light blue smiling eyes and a cheerful personality.

Your Cheating Heart modulated softly to the scratching sound of a worn out record as a few couples danced. Mama, drinking a beer, sat on the end barstool next to the cash register where she took orders for food and beer, while she entertained her customers in her usual profane manner. A customer ask her to give a toast. Mama lifted her beer bottle and announced.

"Here's a toast to all the good rednecks who eat Mama's hamburgers." she heisted the bottle higher. "Here's to the bull what roams in the wood. That does the cows so much good. If it wasn't for the bull and his long red rod. What would we do for meat.—By God." There was a roar of laughter from the customers. They always liked Mama and her crude way of entertaining. Mama's Place normally filled up on Friday and Saturday nights and this night was no exception. There were some men in bib overalls and straw hats sitting at a table near the door.

"I see we have a few farmers in the Place ta'night." Mama said. "Are ya'll from over south-west of Magnolia in the farmin' country?" A loud clamor of recognition came from the table by the door. "Ya'll rednecks down there certainly have my admiration. Let me tell you a little story what bout measures up the height of ya'll folks ambition. It seems there was this shit-eatin' traveling salesman got lost down there on a long loney road. Now ya'll got some roads like that. I know cause I lost my virginity down there on one of 'em. But then, that's another story.—Well, anyway this salesman saw a young boy coming across a big field, so he stopped his car and waited for 'em.

When he got to the road he ask him how far it was to the next town. In the boys slow southern drawl he said. Oh, I'd say bout ten mile, give'er take two'er three."

"Well, the man said. This sure is some lonesome forsaken country. What do ya'll do around here?

"Oh, we hunt and we fuck." the boy said very slowly. The man somewhat taken aback asked the boy what they hunted. In his slow southern drawl he calmly replied. "Sumpin' ta'fuck." Everybody roared with laughter.

By Mama's big Coors clock on the wall it neared midnight and by County ordinance she was to close at twelve o'clock. Everyone knew it and they had begun to disperse as Billy Bob and Effie came in. They went to the end of the bar where Mama was.

"Hey, kid-os, how was the picture show?"

"It was really good Mama." Effie said excitedly. "I want you to go see it. You'll like it."

"Ya'll had a good time, huh?"

"Yes, mam," Billy Bob said. "Really enjoyable. I hope I can call on'er again real soon."

"I spoze that'll be up'ta Effie." Mama said, looking at Effie. With her eyes wide and a smile on her face she quickly shook her head up and down as a positive reaction. "Well" Mama said.

"I guess that means ya'll are, as they say—goin' ta'gether." Effie put her arm around Billy Bob and looked up at him. Both were wearing big smiles. Mama noticed how good they looked together and it pleased her. Billy Bob was dressed casually in light colored slacks and shirt. Effie wore a light blouse with a short dark mini-skirt. Billy Bob decided he should take his leave. He told them bye, thanked Mama again and told Effie he would call her in the morning.

All the customers had left. Mama and Effie were alone. Mama turned off the outside lights. "Why didn't he kiss'ya goodnight?" Mama asked.

"He did, Mama. Before we came in. He figured he could do it more proper if people weren't lookin'."

"Is he a good kisser?"

"Yes'um, he makes me weak and trembly."

"Uh-huh, well you shouldn't ought'ta be wearin' that duck skirt."

"What do'ya mean Mama. Why do'ya call it a duck skirt?"

"You know—Cause it just barely covers the quack."

"Awe, Mama—hush."

Morning came early for Tommy Ray, Arlo and Freeman. The sun had been up for about an hour. The stillness added to the misery of the heat. Tommy Ray and Arlo came out of the trailer house as Freeman drove up in his beat up 1960 Chevrolet Chevelle SS. Mama had, the day before, given Tommy Ray strict instructions about what he had to do today. She had a deadline to meet and the final cooking alone would take three weeks. They had already cooked down three loads of corn and dipped the cobs from the mash after each load. This would be the final load in the big hundred and fifty gallon cooking pot. They would cook it down for three weeks, dip out the cobs, add twenty pounds of yeast and a gallon of shelled and crushed walnuts, cook it all together for another week and then let it ferment for at least three months before starting the condensation process through the copper coils and into the five gallon copper vat. The corn mash would be condensed to sweet thick breath-taking moonshine. Mama was looking at five months to produce five gallons and she had, through a dealer in El Dorado, made arrangements to sell the entire batch to a buyer in Louisiana.

Mama did not know the buyer. Her El Dorado contact made all of the arrangements and would make the delivery, the same as the two preceeding years. This would be the third year for Mama's boys to make moonshine in the still that her daddy made a living from as long as she could remember. She helped him occasionally. Enough to learn about all there was to know about making moonshine. One gallon alone of this uncut moonshine would dilute to approximately forty gallons of one hundred proof pure white lightening. Mama's price for the five gallons of uncut moonshine at fifty percent of it's worth would be twelve thousand dollars. Mama told Tommy Ray to be sure the five gallon butane tank was full so it wouldn't run out before the cooking was done. With four burners under the cooking pot going full blast, it was stretching time to burn for three weeks. He had to remind Mama that he had an extra tank always on standby and that he had already boiled down three loads of corn for this batch. This would be the final load for cooking before they started the fermentation. "Don't fergit the walnuts." she said.

"Mama, let me make the hootch and you tend ta'the business end."

"I want th'motha-fuckin' walnuts in it."

"I know Mama. I know. The walnuts will be in it.—Jessss."

That had been only a little while before Billy Bob showed up and asked Mama if he could date Effie. The devious little wheels in Mama's mind were turning double time as Billy Bob ate his hamburger and talked to her. She seized on and grabbed hold of the presupposed assumption that if the Deputy was to fall in love with Effie, we would have a major player in our court, least there was ever any trouble to come from the law. This had been periodically assaulting Mama's mind since seeing Sheriff Munson snooping around the cornfield and woods along the highway.

CHAPTER 3

Tommy Ray took the red truck with the corn which had yet to be shucked. Arlo and Freeman followed in Freeman's car. The still was only about half a mile through the woods from the back of the cornfield, which they walked only if they didn't have to take anything. Otherwise they had the route set up to confuse anyone who may be snooping around. Mama owned the large tract of woods that the still was in. It and the cornfield, except for the back side of the cornfield were fenced in with posted signs every sixty yards down the highway and around the far end and back of the property. They drove around the back side and down a fence row about three miles to the far corner and through a locked gate. They then drove back down the other side of the same fence for about two miles and veered out into the woods onto a meandering route that crossed itself three times before getting to the still. The still was built on the slope of a large gully above a natural spring. Since there had to be two gallons of water added daily to the mash in the cooking pot, the spring was a Godsend. Nothing could be better than the natural spring water unless it was the gallon of shelled walnuts that Mama insisted on using to give her moonshine a slight hint of a flavor. Mama said it was like the makers autograph. Her daddy had always signed his with pecans.

For about three hours the boys sit on the truck bed shucking corn. Arlo spent most of his time carrying shucked corn in two-gallon buckets up the steps on the side of the cooking pot and pouring it through a hatch in top of the pot. On the ground below he noticed that the old cobs he had dipped out before were gone. "Hey T.R." he called excitedly. "Somebody's been here.

They took the old corncobs!"

"Jessss! Scare th'hell out'ta me. You stupid ass-wipe. The deers ate'em."

Without stopping his shucking or looking up, Freeman began to laugh.

"What'er you laughin' bout. Ya'cocksucker?" Arlo yelled.

"Bout you bein' so fuckin' dumb. Ya'stupid ass-hole."

"How was I spoze ta'know there was deers out here. I bet you didn't know it neither, ya'fuckin bastard. Maybe it weren't deers. Maybe it was one of them big-feeted things."

"Ya'll cut out the stupid horseshit." Tommy Ray said. "If'n ya'got ta'keep talkin', talk about something worthwhile.—Like pussy. By the way Freeman, that reminds me, Mama said ta'tell you if'n you want ta'keep on fuckin' Agnes and Arlene. Ya'got'ta start payin' like everbody else. She said no more free pussy."

"Damn-it. How'd she know I was fuckin' them?"

"Hell, Freeman." Tommy Ray said. "Don't ya'think maybe they told'er. Anyway, Mama seems'ta have a way of knowin' bout everything what goes on around here."

"That's fer damn sure." interjected Arlo.

"Well, ta'hell with it then." Freeman said dejectedly. "I ain't never paid fer a piece of pussy in my life. And I damn sure ain't gona start now."

"Bullshit Freeman." Arlo said. "Don't act so fuckin' high and mighty. Ya'ain't never had none ceptin' from them two whores. Same as me."

"That's beside the point, Arlo. It's high time I started doin' better."

"Hell." Arlo said. "I'm not complainin'. It sure beats the fuck out'ta jackin' off.—T.R., did Mama say anything bout me?"

"Naugh, she didn't mention'ya.—Listen, Arlo, if'n you'll put these last two buckets of corn in'th cooker, and hand me down the buckets, I'll git'th water'ta put in it.Freeman, will you sweep the shucks out'ta the truck bed. We don't want'ta leave a trail through the woods."

"Hey T.R." Arlo said excitedly. "I just figured it out. The reason we always go out and piss around the cornfield.—So's the deers will stay out of it."

"Well God almighty Arlo. There's hope fer'ya yet. Yer beginning'ta smartin' up some."

"Yeah, it makes it stink so bad they won't come near it."

Tommy Ray did not try to explain it to Arlo. He just shook his head from side to side in a despondent manner.

High noon at Mama's Place found Mama, Tommy Ray, Arlo and Freeman having a hamburger, fries and a Coors. There would be no customers showing up before three or four o'clock.

"Mama." Arlo asked. "How come you cut off Freeman's pussy?"

"Arlo." Freeman said. "Damn-it, I can speak fer myself.—Mama, how come you done cut off my pussy?"

"So Freeman." Mama said. "That's why you've been lookin' so down in'th fuckin dumps. God-damn-it boy, if'n it was once in'a fuckin' while, like one fuckin' time a week, it would be al'right. I know you help my boys all the time, and I sure-ly appreciate it. But God-almighty boy, every fuckin' day. Sometime twice a day—both girls. You keep my help plumb worn out. They can't hardly do their work. Much less take on a fuckin' payin' customer.

"Holy Crap." Arlo expounded. "Everyday? God-almighty Freeman, you must be some kin-da' fuckin'—what'cha call it?—whore monger? Damn Freeman, once a week does me plenty fine. Everyday?—Holy Crap."

"Freeman." Mama said. "If'n you think ya'can cut down to just one piece of pussy a week. Then we'll be okay."

"I spoze I'll just have'ta find me a girl friend." he said solemnly.

"Freeman." Mama said. "You're not gona find a fuckin' girl friend what's gona let you hump'er every fuckin' day. You need'ta go see one of them head shrinks, boy.—You've got a fuckin' prob-lem."

"Speakin' of problems." Tommy Ray said. "Mama, don't you think we're inviting one by letting Effie go out with that Deputy Sheriff, with us makin' moonshine. Don't you think she might spill the beans. Ya'know she's out with him again ta'day. I saw'em leavin' when I drove up."

"Sure, I know it. I want'em ta'keep goin' out till he gits so sweet on'er he can't stand it. I've got it planed that way. Anyway, give yer sister a little credit. She knows which side her bread is buttered on. Ain't no way she'd tell'em bout the still.

"What'th fuck you talkin' bout Mama." Arlo said. "If you let'em keep on goin together. Ya'know he's gona be fuckin'er. Then I'll have ta'shoot the cocksucker."

"Now you boys have'ta realize Effie has growed up. She's turned to a woman and ripe fer'th pickin. It will serve a fitting purpose fer us if'n it is Billy Bob what does'th pickin."

"Well, damn-it ta'hell." Freeman said "What about me doin' the pickin". I been eye-balling her sweet little ass for a long fuckin' time."

"Shut the fuck up, Freeman." Tommy Ray said. "Mama's got a plan and I want'ta hear it."

And so, Mama related in detail why she wanted Billy Bob to fall in love with Effie, while Arlo stared detestably at Freeman. His eyes brimmed with feverish hatred.

Effie came in about eleven o'clock, smiled at Mama and said she was going to bed. Mama noticed she looked somewhat flushed but didn't mention it. Effie went into the back to her bedroom and locked the door. Agnes came out with a tray of beer and took it to one of the tables. Most of the rednecks that frequented Mama's Place came to hear Mama's entertainment. Her short toasts, her anecdotes, and sometimes a long story. She was queen of this redneck haven and loved by all. However, there could be those that may come just for Mama's hamburgers. There was no other place in southern Arkansas where one could find a better hamburger. Open face, toasted bun with a hand patted quarter pound of hamburger and all the trimmings including a thick slice of sweet white onion and a generous helping of crispy golden home fries.

At the other end of the room the jukebox played softly. There were always two or three couples slow dancing, feeling each other up. Another Hank Williams song, Cold Cold Heart, issued forth a sad, crying in your beer atmosphere. Mama was surprised to see Vernon Stubbs standing at the other end of the bar. She didn't see him come in. It was as if he just appeared there out of thin air. Vernon was a big tall man. Probably close to seven feet. He wore loose fitting clothes with his trouser length at the top of his enormously big high top brogan shoes. A whisper passed through the crowd referring to him as high-water Pete. No one really knew anything about him or where he hailed from, except Mama, and she didn't know much. He came to Mama's Place only about twice a year. He was always clean shaven with scraggly brown hair, brown eyes and appeared to be around fifty years of age. Mama knew as always that he was going to want to dance with her. And she knew she could not refuse him. She knew Vernon from way back in her partying days. He was her shame, her inner voice, her moral sense, her conscience.

The record on the jukebox changed to a Leroy Van Dyke song, but it was immaterial to Vernon what was playing, he danced the same to any music. He walked down the bar and put his hand out to Mama. Mama pulled a couple of pins out of her hair and let it down. She shook her head to loosen her hair and it fell in waves across her shoulders and partway down her back. Not many of her customers had ever seen her with her hair hanging down. It gave her an erotic and lascivious appearance. Mama took Vernon's hand and he lead her to the dance floor.

"Just walk on by…. wait on the corner…. I love you but we're strangers when we meet" issued forth melodically from the jukebox as Vernon's big oversize clodhoppers hit the floor with a crash. Holding Mama's hands, he backed up from her and bent at the waist to put himself eye-level with her. He shuffled his big feet around, occasionally stomping and hollering "yelp-yelp". The other couples got off the dance floor to give him room as he and Mama shuffled around the floor going through the same stomping and yelping routine a few times. He then straightened up and shuffled his feet in place as he started shaking over his entire body holding Mama close to him. They shook and went through vulgar, lewd and suggestive gestures. The people sitting around the room watched the steamy, provocative dancing, if it could be called dancing, with much sensuality and sexual arousal. The dancing worked as an aphrodisiac to anyone watching.

The shaking gradually turned to twitching before settling into a hard rigorous shimmy. Vernon stood in place and shimmied with Mama following suit. The shimmying along with intermittent twitches was alike to an epileptic seizure. Refered to by the old people as a Saint Vitus dance. This lasted for about ten minutes and slowly came to an end with Vernon and Mama ringing wet with sweat and her thin dress sticking to her body. The local druggist, not caring the least what people thought, sat in his chair by the wall and master-bated. Others were trying to find a hiding place, One couple only made it to the veranda. Agnes and Arlene, each hurriedly lead a male customer to their trailer.

CHAPTER 4

It was a warm, sunny and serene Sunday morning. Mama had biscuts, fried eggs, grits, ham and red-eye gravy on the table in the kitchen and awaited her children. Vernon had left at the break of day to go home, wherever home was. Tommy Ray and Arlo came in through the kitchen door. Sunday morning breakfast was a long standing custom for the Muldunes. It was the time to talk about the past week and plan for the coming one. To get any animosities off their chest and clear up ill wills. Mama poured coffee for the boys as Effie came out of her room and sit at the table. "Tommy Ray" Mama asked. "Do ya'll still get along good with Freeman? I know he's with ya'll all the time and you don't pay him nothing for his help. I was wonderin' if ya'll was always on good terms. Yer grandpa was a smart man, and he always use to say familiarity breeds contempt. So, I was just wonderin'—that's all."

"Mama" Tommy Ray asked without answering her question. "Why did'ya leave the outside lights on all night?" Tommy Ray hardly got the question out of his mouth when there was a banging on the back door. Mama went to the door. Billy Bob talked excitedly. "Mama, mam. Is Tommy Ray and Arlo here? I need'ta see'em real bad." Mama opened the door for him to come in. They were at the table. "I went ta'the trailer. Tommy Ray, I need yall's help. I found the Sheriff hurt real bad down in yall's woods, and I can't handle him by myself."

"Explain what yall was doin' in our fuckin' woods." said Mama.

"Well, mam. I was lookin' fer the Sheriff. You see, it was like this. I was comin' from El Dorado on some early morning' business. And I noticed the Sheriff's car parked a ways off the road on the backside of yall's property. So I stopped to investigate. I hollered fer'em, but got no answer. I noticed a place with the grass all smushed down where it looked like he crossed the fence. So I followed the signs. I found Mister Munson bout maybe a couple hundred yards into the woods. He's layin' by a big hicker-nut tree and he can't move. He's been hurt real bad. The side of his head is hurt and he acts like he's got some busted ribs. He's conscious but he want let me try to move him. He keeps ranting bout something' throwin' him against the tree. I need help to get him to the hospital. I didn't wan'ta call the Sheriff's department in El Dorado to bring an ambulance. And have'm trompin' round all over yall's woods. I thought with Tommy Ray and Arlo's help we could carry him out and take him to the hospital. By the way. I found his shotgun. It was bent in half."

"God-damn." said Arlo.

"Alright, boys." Mama said. "Yall get up off yer ass and go with Billy Bob—He didn't say what is was?"

"No mam, I don't think he saw what it was. He kept sayin' he saw Angie playin' with a little animal and he was slipping up toward her when it happened. Mam, I think he's talkin' out of his mind." Tommy Ray and Arlo got up and said, Let's go. Effie got up and hugged and kissed Billy Bob. They went out the door and to the boys trailer house where Billy Bob's car was. "Hold up, let me get my gun." said Arlo. They pulled up behind the Sheriff's car in record time and brought the Sheriff, screaming in pain out of the woods. And in the Sheriff's car, they took him to the El Dorado hospital.

Mama and Effie got to the hospital as Billy Bob and some interns were taking the Sheriff from the car at the emergency entrance. Some hospital staff put him on a stretcher and rolled him through a set of double doors into the examination room. They would only let Billy Bob go in with him. Mama, Effie and the boys sat in the waiting room. They sat quiet, fuming and waiting. In about twenty minutes Billy Bob came out. "The Doctor sedated him and is going to get x-rays. He said soon as he looked at the x-rays he would talk ta'me."

"Let's go outside." Mama said. "So's we can talk in private." Outside Mama, Billy Bob and Effie sit on an outdoor concrete bench and the boys sit on the ground in front of them. "Now, Billy Bob" Mama asked. "Do you have any idea why Sheriff Munson was in our woods?"

"Yes mam, I think he was probably looking fer a still. He told me that he believed Tommy Ray and Arlo was makin' moonshine. I had no idea he was goin' lookin' fer it. He said they must be, on account of all the corn they growed. I spected it a long time afore he did. But I weren't goin ta'say nothing." *He deduced that this little fib would put him in an altruistic light with Mama.*

"Can you put any light on how he got hurt on that tree?"

"No mam. I can say from lookin' at the new branches on the tree that he hit it about fifteen feet from the ground."

"And his shotgun." Tommy Ray said. "Bent double. Ya'think it might' of been a little tornado or sumpin' like that?"

"What he said about Angie." Arlo said. "What do'ya make of that?"

"He could have fuckin' well seen her." Mama said. "She's been livin' somewhere back there in them woods. I was goin' ta'tell ya'll bout it when Billy Bob knocked on the door. She came ta'see me bout two weeks ago. I hadn't known exactly how ta'tell ya'll yet. She's got a baby boy. Bout two years old. I didn't know it's daddy was with her. That must be what happened ta'the Sheriff. He was protectin' her and the boy." Everyone was in a state of shock at what Mama was saying as she sniffled and slightly shed tears. No one had ever seen Mama cry. "The baby is a cute little guy." she sniffled. "Looks like a real live teddy bear with little humongous feet."

"Good God-damn." exclaimed Arlo. "A big-feeted baby."

"You mean she done took up with a Bigfoot creature Mama?"

"Sure peers like it, Effie. She's got the proof to back it up."

"Then you're grandma to a Bigfoot." sniggered Effie.

"Same as you're an aunt." answered Mama.

Billy Bob went into the hospital and was back out in a short time. "The Doctor says he's in a bad way. Five busted ribs. He said they gona have to operate. One of them has a splinter stickin' in his lung. He also has a broken shoulder and a fractured hip.—and a bad concussion. Looks like ol'Avery is gona be here fer awhile."

Late afternoon, ten miles north of El Dorado, off highway 167, Billy Bob and Effie sat at a table in another redneck dive on the bank of Calion Lake. They were drinking a beer and talking after shooting a few games of pool.

"Ya'know" Billy Bob said. "I been goin' ta'El Dorado early every Sunday morning fer awhile takin' tests at the Sheriff's office so's maybe I could transfer over there. I was comin' back from there when I saw the Sheriff's car parked out by the end of the woods. Looks like now I'll have ta'stay and take care of things in Smackover. What with Avery bein' laid up."

"How come ya'want to transfer down there?"

"Cause I'll make more money there and we can have a better livin' when we get married. You ain't changed yer mind, have'ya?"

"Heck naugh, silly. But I thought you was just sayin' that last night so's ya'could fuck me. Sure, I want'ta marry'ya."

"If'n Mama finds out I've done violated you and taken your virginity. She's gona kill my ass fer sure."

"Shit, Billy Bob. I done lost my virginity way back last year."

Billy Bobs face paled. The only thing he could think of to say was "To who?"

"Not to who" she muttered remorsefully. "But, to what.—T'was a fuckin' cucumber, that's what.—Anyway, if'n you remember right. It weren't you what done the seducing. T'was me. So if'n she figures it out, I'll straighten her out so's she don't kill'ya. I think we better be goin'. It'll be gitten' dark in a'couple of hours and I don't want Mama to be there by herself what with all that's happened ta'day. I need ta'be there ta'kind'a console her. I'm sure glad she don't open up on Sunday like this place." Mama not opening on Sunday had an appreciable amount to do with it being a day of worship. She needed one day a weak off and figured it would be a good day because much of her redneck clientele did go to church.

Billy Bob paid the bill and they went outside to where his old faded 1960 Chevrolet Impala was parked under some big oak trees with other cars. A little further out the lake was rimmed with giant cypress trees in a quaint picturesque panorama. They got in the car and necked a little while before leaving.

Earlier when they had left the hospital. Tommy Ray road back with Billy Bob in the Sheriff's car. They stopped back by the woods and Tommy Ray drove Billy Bob's Impala to Billy Bob's house. Billy Bob left the Sheriff's car and took Tommy Ray home in his Impala. This gave Billy Bob the ideal opportunity to ask Tommy Ray about the still and the corn. "Naugh." he said. "We ain't got no fuckin' still. We sell the corn at the farmer's market in El Dorado. You're not fuckin' my little sister, are'ya?"

Billy Bob looked expressionless at him and did not answer. When they pulled up in front of Mama's Place, Tommy Ray got out and went around the house toward his trailer. Effie came out the front door and got in the car with Billy Bob. On the way across country on highway 335, a meandering two-lane blacktop, through the little town of Norphlet toward highway 167 and on the way to Calion, Billy Bob pulled off the road into the woods and stopped. Effie had on her short duck skirt which offered no resistance in her ability to straddle him on the back seat. She was not nervous like the night before, after enticing him, and then letting him take the initiative. He could tell by the way she trembled that she had never traveled that road before. He was slow and easy and explored her ravishing body in places where there had never been a mans hand before. She wanted so much to become a complete woman, and that night she did.

After about ten minutes of heated, lustful and passionate copulation, they proceeded on to Calion. During all of their time of talking at the Calion beer joint, Billy Bob deliberately avoided asking her about the still. He did not want to put her into a position of having to lie to him.

They took the same route back, passing the big red barn, a local landmark and going by the goat woman's house as they came into Norphlet. She had recently bought ajoining property for her proliferating goats, her babies, as she refered to them. It was said that she had an open window on the back of the house so they could come inside at their fancy. The goat woman was another landmark for an abundance of weirdness in this section of the country. It is said that she was a renowned European concert pianist in her younger days. Go figure, huh.

Billy Bob dropped Effie off and went home to get his thoughts together. He lived with a non-caring drunkard father. His mother had passed away from cancer when he was in high school, accounting for his father's condition. Abner Cross, an oil man and Mayor of Smackover was Billy Bob's uncle on his mother's side. He planned on seeing him tomorrow after going to check on the Sheriff.

Spick-and-span, in uniform, Deputy Sheriff Billy Bob Henry, at 8:30 a.m. at the Union Memorial Hospital, talked to the doctor about the condition and prognosis of Sheriff Avery Munson.

"He underwent extensive surgery and consequently lost his right lung. He's in intensive care and kept sedated. His wife and daughter are in the intensive care waiting room if you wish to speak to them."

"Thank you doctor. Yes, I called them yesterday. I'll stop and see them. Is there anything I can tell them?"

"There is no way at this time that I can give a realistic medical assessment as to the probable outcome. Just tell them to hang in there and hope for the best."

"Thank you doctor. I'll keep checking with you." Billy Bob went and talked to Mrs. Munson and the grown daughter. "All I can say is for us to keep prayin'. When he pulls through from this operation. Then he'll start to improving." Billy Bob left and was at Mama's Place by 10 a.m. Mama, Effie and the boy's were eating breakfast in the front. Mama fixed Billy Bob a plate while Effie poured him some coffee. He took off his hat and surprisingly saw a hatrack on the wall where he put it. "Tommy Ray, I have the Sheriff's shotgun out in the car. I'm goin' ta'give it ta'ya ta'hide and we won't say nothing bout it to nobody else. You hide it real good so's it can't never be found." Tommy Ray nodded his head with an understanding grin. "Mama, mam." Billy Bob asked. "Have'ya heard anything else from Angie?"

"No, but I'm sure I will. Just don't know when."

"I just came from the hospital. The prognosis don't look good. Even if everything go's well. Avery's gona be layed up fer a long time."

"Billy Bob," Effie asked. "You gona be handlin' all the Sheriff'n' now?"

"I don't know yet. I'm goin'ta see the Mayor in a little while. But I spect I will." He began to eat his breakfast. "Mama, mam. This is delicious. Have you taught Effie ta'cook like this?"

Mama immediately caught the fact that Billy Bob was interested in how well Effie could cook and not just that maybe she fucked well. She assumed that he had already found that out. *"What the hell,"* she thought. *"If she hurried it... she comes by it naturally."* Yeah, she said. "Effie cooks real good."

CHAPTER 5

Billy Bob sat in the Mayor's receptionist office, with his hat in his lap, waiting to see the Mayor. In a few minutes a man came out and left. The receptionist said "You may go in now, Mister Henry."

"Thank'ya, mam." Billy Bob said, and entered the Mayor's office. The Mayor stood up and came around his desk with his hand outstretched.

"Hello, Billy Bob. How've you been?"

"I've been great, Uncle Abner. How bout you?" Billy Bob said as they shook hands.

"Well, Billy Bob. Looks as though we have problems. The hospital tells me Avery is in a bad way."

"Yeah, I just came from there. I spoze'ya want me ta'handle things at the office durin' the interim?"

"They say he's gona be layed up fer a long time, Billy Bob. Could be even fer a year or more. That's to long fer a Junior Officer ta'hold down an office as important as the Sheriff's office. What I'm gona do is make you acting Sheriff till Avery can return. I know you can function expertly. Avery has told me numerous times of your ability and dedication. I'll pick up his badge and bars fer'ya. And you git in there and be the Sheriff. He'll understand. Listen, he told me he expected Mama's boys were makin' moonshine. I guess that's why he was in the woods. If'n I was you, I'd turn a deaf ear to that. If'n they are trying to make moonshine. They probably don't know what they're doin' foolin' round with that old fifty year old still. And if'n they did make some. We could never prosecute'em. They being minors. We would git laughed out of court."

"Uncle Abner. You mean there sure nough is a still in them woods?"

"Yeah, their Grandpaw ran moonshine from that still bout all his life.

He raised Mama selling moonshine whiskey. And he helped many a poor families round this country. Kind'a like a Robin Hood, you might

say. And he was a good friend of mine, too. Sometimes a body has to just look the other way. Any-
how, Billy Bob. It would be best not to fret over
them boys and that old still. I'll git your badge in
a couple of days. Then we'll have a little swearing
in at the courthouse, Sheriff Henry. By the way,
how's yer Dad doin. Is he still in the dumps?"

"Yeah, thanks fer askin' Uncle Abner. I'll
make'ya a good Sheriff."

"I know you will, Billy Bob. If'n I didn't think
you would. You wouldn't git the job." They shook
hands again and Billy Bob left thinking, "*The first
thing I'm goin' do when I'm officially Sheriff .... is
requisition a new air conditioner fer the office.*"

It neared noon when Billy Bob pulled up to
Tommy Ray's trailer and tapped his horn. He
had gone home and changed out of his uniform,
put the shotgun in a plastic garbage bag and put
it in his Impala, all the while thinking about the
Bigfoot creature, Angie and Avery. "*It had'ta be
him what slung Avery against that tree. Wonder if
Mama has seen Angie and the little one again.... I
sure would like ta'see that little one .... maybe Effie
might want ta'go riding.*" Arlo stuck his head out
the door, turned and called Tommy Ray. They
both walked out to Billy Bob's car.

"You the same guy what was here before." Arlo jested. "Ya'sure change yer clothes a lot."

"Yep, same one, Arlo. He got out of the car, opened the back door and handed Tommy Ray the sack with the bent shotgun in it. "I forgot ta'leave this earlier. Be sure ya'hide it real good. We don't want anyone ever seein' it."

"Yeah, okay." said Tommy Ray.

"How's Mama doin'. She gona' be al'right?"

"Yeah, she's alright. I tried to git'er not ta'open tonight. But she wouldn't hear of it. She's gona open anyway." Tommy Ray put the sack on the seat of his old red pick-up. "I know just the place for this. I need ta'fix a leanin' fence post on the back side."

"Where?" Arlo asked. "I ain't seen no leanin' fence post."

"That's alright, Arlo. There's lots of things you don't see. I think Effie's in the house. Arlo, go tell'er Billy Bob's here." Arlo sauntered off toward the house. Effie beat him back to the car.

"Hey, Billy Bob. Ya'want'ta go riding."

"Sure, sure." They were in the car and backing out as Freeman drove up in his beat up Chevelle. He looked hatefully at them driving away.

"Why do ya'll keep on letting her go out with that cocksucker?"

"So's you can't keep on eye-ballin' her sweet little ass." Arlo glared with hostility. "You stay round here and you ain't gona be eye-ballin' nothing. Cause I'll shoot yer God-damn fuckin' eye-balls out'ta yer fuckin' head. My gran-paw said you done got to fuckin familiar." Freeman backed out and left. "Guess I told him.—Huh, T.R.?"

"Yeah. Guess you sure-nuff did."

Billy Bob had decided it was high time he and Effie got into a bed. With her up close to him hanging onto his arm, he pulled into an out of the way motel in El Dorado. He drove on past the office and walked back to register. He didn't want them to see how young Effie looked. Like it would make a shit to the manager. Once inside the room Effie grabbed him and threw themselves across the bed. She began kissing him and unbuttoning his shirt. Effie was as hot as a firecracker and wanted to get right to it. Kind of like the proverbial cat on a hot tin roof. Just as Mama had reasoned, she came by it naturally.

Tommy Ray put some tools in the back of the pick-up truck Told Arlo to come with him and they drove down the back fence row about two miles. Tommy Ray, with Arlo's help took the staples from four fence post and layed the four strands of barbed wire back out of the way. The third post, he pushed, pulled and wiggled it, loosening it enough to pull out of the ground. He handed Arlo a shovel from the truck and told him to dig the hole out and make it deeper. When that was done he put the sack with the shotgun in it into the hole and covered the hole up with the dirt, packing it firmly. Then with a post hole digger he reset the post. They restrung the wire pulling it tight and stapling it back to all of the fence posts. They both kicked a bunch of leaves onto the newly exposed dirt and backed up to admire their work.

"A job well done." Arlo grinned. "But I never knew that post was leaning."

"Being as how we are this close." Tommy Ray said. "Let's go on around to the still and put to-day's water in the cooker." He made sure all the tools were in the truck and they drove on around and through the gate. They came back down the fencerow and meandered their route to the still. As they each toted a bucket of water from the spring there came a blood chilling sound from atop the gulley slope. Not loud, just an attention getting course growl. Petrified, they looked up, Arlo fell back dropping his bucket. There on top of the slope was a gigantic brown hairy Bigfoot with Angie in new jeans and a chambray shirt holding his hand on one side and a small Big-foot child holding on to a finger on the other side. Angie was waving at them. She turned loose the Bigfoot's hand and came down the slope. She smiled gleefully and hugged both of them while gesturing up the slope to her family. The baby kept looking up at his daddy and back down at his mama. Angie, simulated pounding her chest like Tarzan, smiled big and threw kisses up the slope. She hugged both boys again, kissed them on the face and quickly scampered back up the slope. She waved bye and they just as quickly disappeared into the woods. Neither of the boys said anything. Arlo filled his bucket back up, they climbed the steps, opened a lid on top of the boiler, poured the water into the boiling mash, got into the pick-up truck and left without talk-ing. They each were dealing with what they wit-nessed in their own individual way. They drove back to the trailer and went inside before Arlo finally spoke. "She peered to be happy." he said. Tommy Ray looked at him. "Yeah, by golly, she did, didn't she."

"T. R. How come people call'er dumb.—She's not dumb."

"They say that cause she can't talk."

"Shit, I know a lot of people that can talk. What's dumber'n she is."

"Yeah, I spoze yer right, Arlo."

"Hey, T.R. Have you ever seen Mama dance?"

"Naugh, don't believe I have. Ya'know, she don't like us going in the Place while she's—Well, you know —performin' fer th'customers. I didn't know she even danced at all."

"You should of seen it. I went in to just ask'er sumpin, and I stood in the door behind the bar and watched. Her and some real tall man were on the dance floor. I spoze ya'could call it dancing. They both were shakin' like a dog shittin' peach seeds. Man it were really sumpin'. Scared'th hell out'ta me. I don't never want'ta see'er do that again."

After the third or fourth concupiscent episode of steamy sex. Not to be confused with love making. Billy Bob decided they should go. He said he had to change clothes and get to work.

"What'cha got ta'do Billy Bob?'

"I got ta'do some Sheriff'n work. Then we got ta'tell Mama we want ta'get married."

"Can't we just run away and get married?"

"No, Baby, we can't. She has to give her approval and sign a paper. You're not thinking she won't do it—are'ya?"

"No, I'm not thinking that. I just don't know how come you have ta'be a Deputy and be so lawful bout it?"

"That's something else I want ta'let yall know. After tomorrow I won't be a Deputy anymore." Effie leaned away from him and looked surprisingly astonished. "I'll be the high Sheriff." Her bemuse quickly did an aboutface to elation. They parked beside the house and went through the kitchen door. Mama, Agnes, and Arlene, were cleaning and readying the Place for opening in another couple of hours. Effie went into her room to clean up.

"Mama." Billy Bob asked politely. "Could we sit down and talk fer a minute?" Mama lead him to the table in the far corner. "What'cha got on yer mind, Billy Bob?"

"Well, first of all. Has Angie been back yet?" He was hedging time and it showed. "No, not yet. What else, Billy Bob?" Mama was enjoying watching him sweat. "What else you want to say."

"I want'ta tell'ya that after tomorrow. I'll be the full fledged high Sheriff of Smackover and, he blurted it out. Me and Effie won't to get married." He sat there grinning ludicrously while Mama stared at him letting him sweat. In a couple of minutes she broke a smile and congratulated him. Effie came in and sit down. "Have'ya ask'er?" Billy Bob held his grin and nodded his head up and down. "What did she say?" Effie asked. He continued to grin and nod his head. "I think something is wrong with him, Effie. Has he ever acted this way before?"

"He's lovesick Mama."

"Is he lovesick. Or just pussy whipped." Mama laughed.

CHAPTER 6

Customers were beginning to pull up into the parking lot. Effie took her Sheriff in the back to her room and locked the door. Tommy Ray and Arlo had retired to their trailer. Agnes and Arlene begin to take orders as the people came in. Mama took her place on the end barstool. A young man came over and sit on a barstool a little way from Mama. "Hey Carl, What'cha want?"

"Nothin' Mama. Just waitin' fer'ya to start talking."

"Tell me, Carl. Have you ever smelled moth balls?"

"Yes, Mam. Grandma keeps some in her trunk."

"Well, tell me Carl. How do you manage to git their little legs spread apart?" He looked dumbfounded at Mama.

"Okay, Carl. That one went over yer head. Whyn't you just sit there and have a beer while you think about it for awhile." All the tables had about filled up. Arlene had started cooking and Agnes continued to take orders and serve beer. "Hey, guys." Mama spoke loud. "I have a cute little story fer'ya. Seems, this young nieve city girl from someplace up north came down south and took a waitress job in a roadside restaurant during huntin' season. Well, hunters would come in every day talking about what they had killed. Then, there were two ardent golfers that would stop by every morning after playing their regular nine holes. One of the golfers always carried two golf balls in his hip pocket. When they sit down he would put the golf balls on the counter to keep from hurting his ass. Now, this young waitress, not knowing hunters from golfers, ask the man what those things were. The golfer told her they were golf balls. The next morning the same exact thing happened. The waitress came by to give them coffee and said. "Oh, I see you killed another golf." There was very little positive reaction. "Not funny, huh." Mama said. "Yeah, I guess it's to long to be funny." Two stools down,

Carl started laughing hysterically. "Did you think that was funny, Carl?" asked Mama.

"I figured it out. Bout the moth balls." and he continued to laugh.

"Mama." someone said. "Sing us a song."

"Yeah." another said. "Sing yer rendition of Red Wings." Red Wings was a very old Indian Intermezzo which was sung with a melody in the style of a Bob Wills Texas swing. Mama got off the stool so she could lead the people in helping her sing the chorus. She began to sing acapella, loud, clear and gleefully.

> "There once was an Indian
> maid....who said she
> wasn't afraid....that some
> little buck... might take a
> fuck...while lying in the
> shade....some little buck
> got wise....and crawled
> between her thighs...and
> with a snoot from his root,
> he opened Red Wings eyes.

Mama began to lead the people in helping her sing the chorus.

> Oh... the moon shines
> tonight...on pretty Red

> Wings… the breeze is
> sighing….the night birds
> crying…Oh… the moon
> shines tonight…on pretty
> Red Wings…while another,
> stills her love away.

"One more time" Mama said as she raised her hands high.

> Ohhhh.. the moon shines
> tonight.. on pretty Red
> Wings….the breeze is
> sighing….the night birds
> crying…Oh… the moon
> shines tonight…on pretty
> Red Wings…while another.
> stills her love away..

Everyone stopped singing, thinking the song had ended.

Then much to her surprise,

Mama continued.

> her belly began to rise….
> and from her cunt…
> came a cross-eyed runt…
> with cobwebs in his eyes..

"Everybody now." Mama conducted with her hands.

> Ohhhhhh.......
> the moon shines tonight...
> on pretty Red Wings...
> the breeze is sighing...
> the night birds crying...

> Oh....the moon shines
> tonight...on pretty Red
> Wings...while another...
> stills her love away...
> while another...
> stills her love away...."

Red Wings, represented a prime paragon of Redneck jovialness at Mama's Place.

"Alright. listen up. Here's one fer anybody what's ever thought about being incestuous. Seems, this young teenage boy was in low spirits cause he couldn't find a job. He was moping round the house, looking all depressed. His dad inquired as to his problem. He told him his girl friend busted up with him, and he was broke and horney. His dad gave him twenty dollars and told him to go down across the tracks where the hookers hung out and buy his self a piece of pussy. On his way down there he had to pass his grandmothers house. So he stopped in to git a drink of water and told her what he was gona do. She told him that was to much money to throw away like that. She said you give me the money and I'll give you some pussy. So, he was across the bed porking his grandma and his dad walked in. His dad hit the ceiling, mad as six wet hens. He pulled him off of her and knocked him down. "Where the hell do you git off fuckin my mama." he yelled.

"Well, damn-it all Paw, I don't see how come you're gittin' so God awful mad bout me fuckin' your mama. You fuck my mama all the damn time."

Mama sit back up on her stool feeling like that one kind of bombed. She picked up her beer and held the bottle high. "Here's a toast fer all the guys everywhere what might be named Kent.— There was a man named Kent. His was so long, it bent. To save time and trouble. He put it in double, and instead of cumin—he went." That was much better as witnessed by loud applause and shouting. It somewhat renewed Mama's self-confidence.

Everything continued normally in accordance with Redneck standards as summer proved it's existence daily with near 100 degree temperatures and humidity almost to match. Billy Bob had been sworn in and had a new air conditioner put in the Sheriff's office. He buckled down to work, staying busy mostly running all over town answering calls to quell family disturbances. He reckoned it was the scorching weather that caused short fuses. Tommy Ray and Arlo had added the yeast and chopped walnuts, cooked it into the mash and started the fermentation process. Tommy Ray was now harvesting his hemp, stripping the leaves and flowers and saving seed for propagating in the new hothouse he was building behind the storehouse. The plants were in the center of the thick corn field in spaces he had cleared between corn stalks. They were high grade Acapulco Gold and he was saving all the seed he could for a bigger crop in the 20 by 40 hothouse. Four of the plants were not yet ready, so he left them for later.

For almost two months no one had seen anything of Angie and her hairy family. Mama was assured that she was still in the vicinity because she had let her know she would be back. No, the boys did not want to go looking for them. The doctors were saying that Avery Munson was not responding as he should and the prognosis was bleak for a full recovery. They said he hallucinated a lot and talked out of his head. He said

Angie was a witch. He said she raised her hands above her head and looked wildly at him. He said he raised swiftly into the air and slammed into a tree. Angie did it, he said. She's a witch. The doctors said it was hallucinations brought on by trauma. Billy Bob visited him every three or four days, usually with an apple which he peeled for him.

Effie, stayed in her room and suffered from a syndrome of melancholy. Brought on by worrying about her period being late. Mama had mixed feelings about Effie's predicament. She would certainly welcome a regular or human-kind grandchild, maybe even three or four. She secretly contemplated having a talk with Billy Bob about keeping Effie knocked up and bare-foot until she had a house full of kids. *"She needs them to keep her busy."* she thought as a devilish smirk crept across her face. "Effie." she called out from the kitchen. "We all better go to the court-house tomorrow and get ya'll hitched up.

"Alright Mama, I'll tell Billy Bob when he comes by this evening."

There came a light knocking on the back door. Mama opened the door and there they were. Angie and the child. Angie smiled and motioned for Mama to come outside. Mama looked out toward the woods for her man, creature, mate or whatever he should be called. There he was out by the side of the cornfield. Mama knew that was why she wouldn't come in. He had to be able to see her and the boy. Mama called for Effie and told her Angie was here. She came out of her room and out the door with Mama. There was beautiful sisterly jubilation when they saw one another. Hugging and dancing around. Effie sit on the bottom step and held out her arms toward the child. He looked at his mama for her approval. She nudged him toward Effie. Effie put her arms around him and hugged him. He again looked at Angie for assurance. She smiled at him and nodded. The child then put his little arms around her and hugged her. Effie cried happily. He was like a soft live little teddy bear. She had a fleeting thought of wanting to keep him which augmented the hope that she was pregnant. She looked out toward the cornfield and saw the huge creature. A cold shiver went up her spine. The Bigfoot had pulled a couple of ears of corn that had been missed and was eating them while he kept his eyes on Effie and the child. She played with the child while Angie and Mama communicated. Silently of course. The child held Effie's blonde hair across his fingers, looked at it and smiled at her. He liked her hair. He also liked her breasts. He felt of them and tried to open her blouse.

She could not but help but notice his wide little mouth with the big thick teeth. *"My God"* she thought, *"Does Angie still nurse this kid. Surely not…. Good Lord"* and she shuddered.

Angie took the boy by the hand, Effie got up and they all hugged again. Mama stooped over and hugged the child. Angie and the child then went out to where the creature waited. He picked them up, gently putting one astraddle each hip, and disappeared in long fast strides down the fence row, across the field and into the far back woods. Mama looked at Effie with watery eyes. "They're gone fer good this time." she said.

"Ya'mean they ain't never comin' back?"

"Looks that way." Mama's voice quivered. She said they were going north to the mountains. She indicated there were others. Like a tribe of relatives or something. Anyway, they're headed fer the mountains." That morning by the back steps Mama and Effie hugged affectionately and cried.

CHAPTER 7

It was after Tommy Ray and Arlo had breakfast with Mama and Effie that they decided to
go check things out at the still. "Let me get my
shotgun." said Arlo. Then they walked along the
backside of the cornfield to the woods, crossed
the fence and proceeded on to the still. "What
we goin' ta'the still fer, T.R.?

"Jus' checkin' ta'be sure everything is alright."

"Reckon we might see Angie?"

"Weren't you listenin' when Mama said they
was gone?"

"Oh, yeah."

Upon nearing the still they heard a chopping
sound and creeped up to the edge of the gulley
across from the still to see Freeman, with a dou-

ble blade axe, starting to chop down the steps from the side of the boiler.

"What the fuck you think you're doin" yelled Tommy Ray, as Arlo half sliding, scampered down the embankment to a position directly across from Freeman. Freeman, started to run up the embankment on the other side toward his car. He fell, got up and slung the axe at Arlo. With the axe swishing through the air, Arlo shot as he dodged it. Freeman fell with an excruciating scream and rolled to the bottom of the gulley. He lay about twelve feet from the spring bleeding profusely when Tommy Ray reached him. Arlo never got up. He sat where he shot from. Tommy Ray looked up at him. "God-damn, Arlo." he said. "Did'ya have'ta kill'em. What th'fuck we gona do now. Why didn't ya'shoot'em in the legs?" Freeman was hit in the upper left chest region and neck. His neck was half shot away. "I couldn't tell where I was shooting." Arlo said. "I was dodging that fuckin' axe and I just shot."

"Well, we gotta figure out what th'fuck we gona do." Tommy Ray said as he climbed the embankment and sit down by Arlo. "Are you alright, that axe didn't hit'ya, did it?"

"Naugh, I'm alright."

Tommy Ray and Arlo sat on the gully embankment for at least an hour looking down at

Freeman and occasionally glancing at each other. Tommy Ray put his head in his hands and was motionless for another half an hour. Arlo thought he had gone to sleep when all of a sudden he looked at Arlo, scaring him, and said "I've got it."

"What do'ya got?" asked Arlo.

"A plan. What we're gona do. Come on, I'll explain it to'ya while we do it." Arlo followed Tommy Ray down to where Freeman lay. "Now, put yer gun down and let's drag'em up to his car." They each took a leg and began climbing and dragging Freeman up the embankment to his car. It was tedious going but they made it. They pulled Freeman into the back seat of his car. Arlo had brought the axe and laid it down with his shotgun. Tommy Ray checked for the car keys. They were in the ignition. He told Arlo to get his shotgun and the axe. He then put the axe in the back with Freeman. They got in the car and drove out to the gate where Tommy Ray did some powerful swearing about the gate being knocked down. Freeman had just run through it knocking it off it's hinges. "We'll have ta'come down here tomorrow and put it back up." Tommy Ray said. "I'm glad ya'killed the cocksucker, Arlo." Arlo looked at him and grinned. "Yeah." he said. "The sons-a-bitch ain't gona be eye-ballin' her sweet little ass no more. Just goes ta'show'ya, T.R.—a motha-fucker can get killed fer reckless eye-ballin'.

"Arlo" Tommy Ray said. "That eye-ballin' bull-shit has really been botherin' you, hadn't it."

"Not no more—it ain't."

"Yeah, I reckon not.—Now, what we're gona do is go to the house just long enough ta'git the truck. I'll git something out of the storehouse ta'cover'em up. I want you ta'git in the truck and follow me. We'll come back this way and go out to the new highway. Then we'll go to the Heaven turnoff. We'll go through Heaven and out the old highway to where we can find a good place to turn out into the swamp. Ya'know all the talk about the wild hogs in that swamp. How the food source is starting ta'run out. And how they say people go out into them woods around the swamp and don't come back. They think them wild hogs are eating'em.—Well, we gona let them fuckin' hogs have ol'Freeman."

"Yeah." Arlo grinned.

Arlo followed Tommy Ray as instructed. About ten miles out the highway they turned off to the right on the old highway 7. The narrow road twisted and turned through the woods a few miles until suddenly around a curve, loomed a sign. HEAVEN-pop. 1250.

About 500 yards past the sign, on the right, sitting back from the road was an old farm house, with a big shed and a number of hog pens, behind it. Just past the house the road forked and the old highway continued to the left. Another sign with an arrow and the name HEAVEN, pointing to the right. Tommy Ray turned right as Arlo followed in the truck. They continued down Main street which ran parallel to old highway 7, a half mile to the north, and back out to the old highway one mile past town. The old highway continued another four miles before intersecting the new highway. The town embodied a various abundance of large hardwood trees. Was made up of many two story structures of ancient brick intermingled with newer wooden structures, and a few old anti-bellum homes. Heaven had a history dating back before the Civil War. It was one of the oldest towns in the area and had thrived and grown. Going through town, they passed through two over-hanging traffic lights, a Texaco station and a school house. Less than a mile west of town, before they came back out to the old highway 7, they passed a large trailer park community. Back on the old highway 7, Tommy Ray began to look for a likely place to turn off. He slowly passed a mailbox with the name Abbott on it. The road looked well used. He didn't want to go up to a house. He kept going. About another mile was a box with the name McGuire on it. He could see the house. It looked like it was vacant. Weeds and vines were growed up around it. He turned in and drove on past the house. Arlo followed in the pick-up truck.After crossing a field, they drove on out into the woods until the ground started to get mushy. Tommy Ray stopped and told Arlo to leave the truck and come with him. "Bring yer gun." he said. They drove Freeman's car into the swampy woods as far as it would go. It began to bog up and stalled. They got out, took Freeman out and dragged him about forty feet further into the woods. Tommy Ray then made sure he left the keys in the ignition and the drivers door open. He took the axe with him. They began to walk back to the truck when four large boars intercepted them emitting horrendous bloodcurdling sounds. Terror-stricken they froze. The frenzied hogs with their chilling snorting started to charge them. Arlo, unconscious of his actions, raised the shotgun and fired at them. They dispersed just long enough for Tommy Ray and Arlo to make it to the truck.

Back out of the woods, Tommy Ray turned to the right and intercepted the new highway about four miles up the road. He crossed over to the far side, made a left and headed home. Nothing was said until they pulled up to their trailer. "I bet'cha." Arlo said. "That ol' Freeman's done been ate up by now."

"I bet'cha yer right." said Tommy Ray.

"What'cha want ta'do now T.R.?"

"We need ta'go fix that gate. But first I think I'll dry some weed in the oven."

"Yeah."

As they started to go into the trailer Billy Bob pulled up in the Sheriff's car and got out. "Hey, Tommy Ray. Hey, Arlo, how ya'll doin?"

"We're doin good, Billy Bob. What's up?" asked Tommy Ray.

"Have ya'll seen anything of Freeman?"

Tommy Ray's heart jumped up in his throat, but he controlled the sudden anxiety. "Naugh" he said. "We kinda had a fallin' out and he quit comin' round."

"Yeah, Arlo said. "I think he might'of went ta'work fer Walmart or sumpin." Tommy Ray held his breath in fear as Arlo talked. "What'cha need with'em? Tommy Ray asked.

"It ain't nothing ta'worry bout. A man called me from the Federal Bureau of Alcohol, Tobacco and Firearms, up in Little Rock. He said a State Trooper called him and said Freeman told him about an illegal whiskey still out in the woods. Said he was just trying ta'reach Freeman ta'follow through on it. Said he wanted ta'collaborate his story. Alright guys, if'n ya'see him. Tell'em ta'come see me." He reflected momentarily on what he had just told them and retracted. "Never mind, I reckon ya'll won't be seein' him no more, since he tried ta'rat out on'ya." He got in the car, backed up, turned around and left. Later in the day he intended to change clothes and cars and come back to see Effie.

"So." Arlo said. "Ol' Freeman's been talkin' out of school. I should of shot the cocksucker two days ago. Should of knowed he'd be makin' trouble. If'n I didn't think the dick-head, pretty little ass, eye-ballin' sex fiend, whore mongerin' bastard weren't already ate up. I'd go out there and shoot his rotten ass again."

"Jesus Christ, Arlo. Ya'got kinda wound up there, didn't'ya. Come on, let's go in and dry some weed."

"Yeah, and get high."

CHAPTER 8

Morning found Tommy Ray and Arlo working on the gate. Mama, Effie and Billy Bob were at the courthouse. The same Judge that swore Billy Bob in as Sheriff had now married him to Effie. Mama dabbed at her eyes with a small lace hanky. Only because that was what mothers did in movies. She certainly wasn't weeping. On the contrary, she was ecstatic. The Judge wished them well and they went back to Mama's Place in her big nineteen sixty Fleetwood Limousine. No one talked. Effie still had not started her period. *"I'll let her tell him in her sweet time"* Mama thought. *"Maybe I want have to have that talk with Billy Bob....They will probably have a house full without my coaxing."*

Mama made them a hamburger while Effie packed some things to take to her new home. Billy Bob told Mama about the call from the ATF man and told her not to worry. He would squash it as best he could. Mama told him she was going to close the Place for the next couple of weeks due to the oil celebration. She discovered last night that her attendance had dropped to almost nothing. It had been the opening day for the gigantic Arkansas Semi- Centennial Oil Celebration taking place at the fair grounds in El Dorado. And it was to run for two weeks. Mama had never before closed except on Sundays and she certainly didn't want to now, but she couldn't fight it. There was no use opening to an empty house.

El Dorado and Smackover alike had put a lot of effort into the celebration. The El Dorado fair grounds was made to represent the original old boomtown of the twenties. An old passenger train was at great expense hauled in to run on a track surrounding the fairground. A big derrick was constructed and places of business operated along the street including a saloon and brothel. Three frilly and colorfully dressed ladies of the night stood on the balcony over the saloon enticing customers to come up. A cowboy, in full rough cowboy attire and a six gun on his hip called up to them and asked how much they charged. One of the ladies called back down. "A quarter." A meek little man in the crowd broke away from his wife and headed for the saloon door. His wife caught him at the door, pulled him back, and continued on up the street. The cowboy was one of five stuntmen which were brought in from Hollywood to put on stunt shows like robbing the train, getting shot off their horse while trying to get away from a bank robbery. Staging a hanging and various other things. The fair ground was packed with people every night. Mama's Place didn't have a chance of getting customers until the celebration ended. Tommy Ray and Arlo saw Billy Bob and Effie out there one night. "Look there at Billy Bob." Arlo said. "Whyn't we beat the fuck out'ta him."

"Damn, Arlo. He's yer brother-in-law. You know they're hitched."

"We could take'em out and shoot'em and feed his Sheriffing ass ta'the fuckin' hogs."

"God-damn-it, Arlo. Don't you ever fuckin mention nothing like that again. Ya'want'ta git us put in jail.—Jessss."

"I was just funning. T.R. Don't git all riled up." He hollered at Billy Bob and Effie. They waved and went over to see them. "Hey, brother-in-law." Arlo said and shook his hand. "Ya'll having fun." Effie hugged both her brothers. "Did ya'll see that man git shot of his horse a while ago." she asked. "Yeah, we saw it." said Tommy Ray.

"Shit." Arlo said. "It weren't nothing. I could do that."

So, after the oil celebration had ended. Time advanced at a seemingly rapid pace. Mama continued to entertain her customers, but didn't seem to show as much enthusiasm as before. Her mind was preoccupied on a hypothetical supposition which began developing while she watched some comedy store shows on television. It had now came to an exacting reality in her mind. She was going to enlarge the Place, put in a small stage with spotlight, mike and stool, install a sound system and have open mike three or four nights a week. It would give the Place a shot in the arm that it really needed. She had been having the feeling that she was losing her appeal telling the same stories over and over. So, let some new talent do some entertaining for her. *"Why not,"* she thought.

Effie's period never started. She was now showing quite significantly in being with child. Billy Bob was as proud as a peacock and his dad was doing better since Effie moved in. He would now get out of his recliner and go to the table to eat. Tommy Ray and Arlo stayed high and happy. They had finished the hothouse and had thirty small plants ready for transplanting into three rows of large pots. Billy Bob had again just recently talked to Lieutenant Stewart at the Bureau of ATF. He told him that Freeman Blankenship had undoubtedly left the area and that he should put no credence in anything he had said. He told him Freeman had always been a lair and troublemaker. The Lieutenant said he would pass the information on along to the Captain.

Avery Munson was still in a non-recovery mode. He lay strapped up in his bed mumbling incoherently and constantly being sedated. The doctors said he was slowly healing physically but regressing mentally.

Mama began to put her plan into action. She called "Harold" a local contractor whom had worked for her before. He came out that same morning and Mama explained to him what she had in mind. She wanted the entire varanda removed and the front of the house extended out thirty feet all the way across. She would leave the dance floor area as is and have a divider wall behind it making a thirty foot nook between the outer wall and the dance floor. Then she wanted a two foot riser stage about nine by fourteen feet put in the center of the room against the south wall. For décor she wanted the stage to appear as a front porch with a fake window and door on the back wall. She would leave it up to Harold to have the sound system and lighting installed. "Once the addition is complete." she told Harold. "Put the veranda back across the entire front of the house and put the sign back up. And Harold, get enough help so's you can stay on it and git it done as quick as possible. I don't want ta'be shut down no longer than I have to."

Mama opened that night to a full house. She, Agnes and Arlene stayed extremely busy. She was having trouble trying to entertain her customers and keep up with all that had to be done. She told them a drawn out story about a foo bird. The story lost it's interest before reaching the punch line. A heckler spoke up quite load. "What's a matter Mama. That the best ya'can do?"

"Sir," Mama asked. "Have you ever seen an ass-hole wrapped in plastic?"

"No Mama. Don't believe I have."

"Take out yer drivers licence and look at it." The crowd roared.

"Seems, there was this Yankee came down south and bought him a forty acre farm. Out back was a four hole outhouse. He used it for a few months and tired of it. So he had an indoor bathroom put in. A Mexican family came along loaded down with all they owned on top of their old car.

The Mexican asked the man about renting the little house. He told him it was just an outhouse. But he insisted that he would like to rent it. He told him he would pay him fifty dollars a month, three months in advance. "*Fuckin' dumb Mexican*," the Yankee thought, and took his money. The Mexican put a television antena on top of the outhouse and moved in. After about two months went by the man noticed a second antenna on the outhouse and a big Lincoln parked by it. There were more kids running around playing. He asked about it. The Mexican told him he had sub-leased the basement. Mama got very little laughter from that one. She took a couple of hamburger plates to a table and then she continued. "What about them two fuckin' cannibals what killed a man out in the jungle. They knew if they took him to the village they would have to cook him and share with the whole tribe. One cannibal said. "Let's just eat him here. We can eat him raw." So they started on each end. One ate his ears and cheeks off and started on his lips. He raised up and asked. "How you doing down there. "Just great" the other cannibal said. "I'm having a ball." The laughter again was mediocre. Mama raised her hands. "Ya'll all listen up now. I have an important announcement. Starting tomorrow, Mama's Place will be closed awhile fer construction. We're goin'ta'do some remodeling and enlarge the building. So ya'll be sure and watch fer the re-opening. Ya'll will be surprised and delighted at the new Mama's Place. We're gona have a bigger room and a stage over here (she indicated with her arm) with a microphone and spotlight. A few nights a week we will have open mike night, so's ya'll or yer friends can show off yer talents. If'n any of you can play the guitar and sing. It'll be a good time and place fer'ya ta'do it front of an audience."

Early the next morning, Harold and six men dismantled the veranda and placed it in sections out front so it could be reconstructed exactly the same. They had it done in record time and started construction on the a-frame extension of the house bringing it out thirty feet. By the end of the first day the new a-frame was up and the new flooring was laid where the old veranda floor had been. Harold told Mama they would be back in the morning and put the roofing on before they moved the outer wall to the front. Mama was more than pleased with the progress. Effie had spent the day with her, lounging around and talking in her bedroom which Mama had taken over. Effie was excited about what Mama was doing to the Place. She told Mama if she could find a really good folk or country singer she probably could get the radio station to come out and put him or her on the air. "Yeah." Mama said. "That would really be good advertisement too." *"Leave it up to the young-uns to come up with the good ideas."* Mama thought. "Tell'ya what, Effie. Whyn't me and you go to Walmart tomorrow and do some baby shoppin'. There's all kind'a things you are gona' be needing." Mama knew Effie would not be having a shower. She had friends at school but they never visited with her at home. Their parents wouldn't let them come to her house. Mama understood why and she felt bad about it. So she always tried in her own way to make it up to her. "I'll be doin the payin'. So you don't need ta'bring no money."

"Okay Mama. I'll be here bout eight. Is that to early?"

"That's good. I'll be ready ta'go."

"Thank'ya Mama. I sure do preciate it. Ya'know I love'ya."

"I know it child. I love ya'too."

Harold's workers had the plywood up and was laying tarpaper when Billy Bob dropped Effie off. Mama had her car backed out and was watching the work. Billy Bob waved to her and she returned the wave as Effie got into her car. Mama got in and they headed for a big shopping spree at Walmart. Mama could not help but notice the state trooper stopped on the road and looking out across the cornfield. She said nothing about it to Effie. They finished their shopping and had dinner at the Town House before she took Effie home and helped her into the house with all the sacks and packages. She greeted Mister Shaw. He returned her greeting but remained in his recliner.

When Mama got home she went out to the boys trailer. They were working in the hothouse but heard her when she called them. "Listen up now" Mama said. "There's something I want ya'll ta'do. I know it's not time yet fer the fermenting ta'be finished. But I want'ya to see if ya'can drain any shine off yet. If'n ya'do get any. I want'ya to hide it real good so's it want be found. I'm still afraid that them ATF people might come snoopin' round."

"Alright Mama" Tommy Ray said. "We'll go check it right now."

"Yeah." Arlo said. "I bet we can find a leanin' fence post."

Mama looked at him inquisitively but let it drop. "You know if they come out here and want ta'look around, we can't stop'em. Their Federal G-men, kind of like the FBI. They can do what ever the fuck they want to. So boys, tell me. What're ya'll gona do bout that fuckin' hot house?"

"Well, fer God-damn" Tommy Ray said dejectedly. "Shit-fire—maybe they won't come Mama."

Mama walked away shaking her head indignantly. "I certainly the fuck hope not. Go on and see bout the hootch."

CHAPTER 9

Nothing holds back time. It progresses uninter-
rupted awaiting the phlegmatic procrastination
of no one. Time had come and gone for Tommy
Ray and Arlo to drain the condensation from the
copper vat. They retrieved four beautiful amber
tinted gallons of uncut pure moonshine. The
first almost full gallon had long before been hidden as Mama had told them to do. Tommy Ray
put the four gallons in one gallon plastic milk
jugs with blue screw on tops in a box and into
the trunk of Mama's car. She told him to leave
the other gallon hidden for awhile. She wasn't
sure of the proof of it due to it being drained
earlier than it should have. She said they would
check it out later. She took the four gallons to
her contact in El Dorado. Effie was now due in

another six weeks. Everyone was looking forward to the baby boy's arrival. The building had been finished for four months and was a great success. There was a mixer for plugging in other mikes and instruments and a big speaker on either side of the stage. It was fixed so the house lights could be dimmed and a spotlight be on the entertainer. It turned out that there were more singers than comedians. But the customers seemed to like it better that way. Saturday nights were reserved for professional entertainers that Mama paid to perform. She charged a ticket price to help pay the performer and sold reserved tickets in advance which she had printed for each performer. The entertainers that Mama booked were performers that the audience had to sit and listen to. She had lined up eight entertainers through a booking service out of Memphis and each would do a repeat performance (or back by popular demand) every eight weeks at which time she would start booking a new one each month. This Saturday a young man out of Memphis was scheduled to perform songs made famous by the legendary singing brakeman, Jimmy Rodgers. Some of the songs that Jimmy Rodgers is known for include, Soldier's Sweetheart, Blue Yodel (T for Texas), In The Jailhouse Now, Waiting For A Train, My Blue Eyed Jane, Mule Skinner Blues, Blue Yodel

No.3 (She's Long, She's Tall), and My Good Gal's Gone Blues. Plus many many more. Mama's new house with smaller tables and more chairs seats seventy people. By putting tables and chairs on the dance floor she can seat about ten or twelve more. Mama guarantees her performers four hundred dollars for the night and she charges ten dollars for a reserved ticket. She had a sold out house for the next two Saturdays. The following Saturday after the Jimmy Rodgers singer will be a young female Bluegrass/blues/country/folksinger by the name of Melissa Marie Lebeaux and hails from down around Thibodaux, Louisiana. It is said that she is destined to become a superstar. The preceding four Saturdays were sold out houses to a masterful Hank Williams impersonator, a country singer that imitated country stars in action and voice, two young brothers that had an act of singing and talking alike to that of the old Smothers brothers television show. An Elvis Presley impersonator who had his own background music and backup singers electronically plugged into the sound mixer. He did a magnificent job of actually making the audience believe he was Elvis.

For the Saturday performances Mama had a little podium just inside the front door where she checked reservations and took the tickets.

Every Saturday there were a few people showed up without reservations. Mama would take their money and seat them on the dance floor. She put Tommy Ray and Arlo to work. Tommy Ray did the cooking. It seemed to work out to be about fifty hamburgers sold each Saturday plus a whole lot of beer. Mama worked the cash register and introduced the talent. Arlo took care of the lighting from a switching panel set up behind the bar and helped Agnes and Arlene wait tables. Effie wanted to help but Mama said no. "If'n I had a little pregnant girl workin' in here, the people would hang me by my balls." she said.

"Aw Mama. You don't have no balls." replied Effie.

"Just a figure of speech, child. Ya'know what I meant."

Billy Bob did however offer to bring the talent from the El Dorado Holiday Inn each week. He got approval from the Mayor to use the Sheriff's car for transporting them. All was going well for Mama's new enterprise. Mama's Place was the envy of every night club across southern Arkansas. But her act was refined only for those gloriously proficient Saturday nights.

Mama stepped up to the mike amid a steady buzz of talk from the crowded room. She scratched a spoon across the mike making a loud screeching sound. "Ladies and Gentlemen." she said. "Welcome to Mamas Place. We are delighted you could come. I want to ask you to respect your neighbors, and refrain from talking while Mister Rogers sings.—And now, let's all give Mister Jimmy Rodgers Ellsworth a big Mama's Place welcome." The room applauded as a gangly young man dressed in railroad overalls and cap came through the kitchen door and onto the stage. He put his thin guitar rope (he did not have a strap) over his shoulder and stepped up to the mike. "Hello, I'm Jimmy Rodgers." he said and started strumming the guitar interspaced with a few bass runs. He then sang.

> "T…for Texas…T…for
> Tennessee…T… for
> Thelma…. the gal that
> made a wreck out of me….
> YE..O..D..LAY..DEE..
> O..D..LAY..DEE..
> O..D..LAY..DEE….
> D..O..D..E..E..E.."

The young man went on to sing and yodel his way through song after song for two crowd pleasing hours which included one fifteen minute break. Another highly successful night at the renowned Mama's Place.

Mama cheerfully settled with Jimmy and told him she would look forward to a return visit in about two months. Billy Bob took him back to El Dorado and inquired as to where he went from here. He told him he would be in Ruston for a Monday show and Shreveport for Wednesday through Saturday. He was normally booked for four nights a week, sometimes five.

After everyone had left, Mama turned the outside lights off. Being that the next day was Sunday, they as usual, left all of the cleaning for morning. They were all extremely tired and ready to go to bed. "Mama" Tommy Ray asked. "Don't'cha make enough money that'ya could hire a couple more girls ta'help out on Saturday nights?"

"Yeah, I spoze so—let's see, long as we keep fillin' up the house. We make three hundred above what we pay the talent. Plus usually bout another hundred on people we put on the dance floor. And the hamburgers. Bout fifty at five dollars is two fifty—less cost—would make it bout two stead of two fifty—that makes five fifty plus the beer. I don't know what we make on it. But it's a lot.—Yeah, I spoze we could get a couple more waitresses. Mama's record keeping and tallying accounts in her head was something to be desired.

"Ya'gona git young pretty'uns Mama." asked Arlo.

"Could be, son. But they gona be fer waitres-sin'. Not fer fuckin'."

"I weren't thinking' bout that." said Arlo.

"Bullshit." interjected Tommy Ray.

"Ya'll git the fuck out'ta here and go to bed." Mama said. "I'll have breakfast ready at eight o'clock. Then we got'ta clean this place real good and mop the floors."

Agnes and Arlene had breakfast with Mama and the boys. Mama had invited them to be sure they were there to help clean up. They had gotten well into the cleaning in the big room when Mama's El Dorado contact came by and gave her ninety six one hundred dollar bills. He told her he believed he should get his regular five hundred dollar cut even though it was only four gallons instead of five. Mama happily gave him six hundred just to show where her priorities lay. She then ask him to see if he might could find her two girls who would like to work about three hours on Satur-day nights as waitresses. She said she would make up for the short hours with extra pay and be sure they are at least twenty-one. He said he would see what he could do.

Monday night…

> "There once was an Indian
> maid…who said she wasn't
> afraid…that some little buck
> might take a fuck…
> while lying in the shade…."

Mama, on stage, with Red Wings, had kicked off another five nights of unpolished, crass, crude and vulgar entertainment while awaiting the next stupendously virtuous Saturday night.

"Have ya'll folks heard about the man what stopped and filled up his car with gas. He asked the attendant about the big sign on the station what said. Free sex with fill up. The attendant told him it was kind of like a lottery. He said ya'have'ta guess the right number from one ta'ten ta'win. Then he asked him his number. Seven, the man said. Aughh, the attendant said. You were so close. The number was six. The man drove on down ta'the pool hall where he saw a friend of his. He said, ya'know that sign about free sex on that gas station. I think the game is rigged so's ya'can't win. No, his friend said. I know fer a fact it's on the up and up. My wife's done won two weeks in'a row." There was a mediocre applause so Mama reminded them to be sure and get their tickets for next Saturday nights show and plugged the young lady that would be singing. Saying how she had been packing'em in every where she sang. "How did'ya like Jimmy Rodgers the other night?" There was a loud clamor of favorable gratification. Mama was pleased.

CHAPTER 10

Division 14, Federal Bureau of Alcohol, Tobacco and Firearms. Little Rock, Arkansas. "Yes Sir, Captain." Lieutenant Stewart said. "I was reviewing this situation down south, about the illegal whiskey still, you remember it was called in by a State Trooper. Badge number 414. There are a couple of incriminating circumstances which I would like to point out to you."

"Go ahead, Lieutenant." said the Captain.

"Yes Sir, As you know, I tried to contact the man which told the officer about the still, a—lets see now. He looked through his report.

"Oh yes,—a Freeman Blankenship. I even called the local Sheriff to try and contact him. I traced down the name to an address and phone number. I talked to his widowed mother. She

93

couldn't put any light on where he was. She said he was nineteen years old and worthless as tits on a boar. But she said it wasn't like him to just leave. Now, get this. That local Sheriff told me he had disappeared and I shouldn't put any credence in anything he might have told the Trooper. Now Captain, does that not have a ring of foul play to you. And sir, the Trooper called me back again and said he found a patch of marijuana plants in the middle of a cornfield next to the woods with the alleged still."

The Captain looked apprehensively at the Lieutenant for awhile before he spoke. "Stewart, I'm sure you realize that we're on thin ice right now. We're commissioned only to keep abreast of and look for anti-American activities, movements and cults such as young Nazis, fascist, white supremacist or any group which may be stock piling arms At this point in time with a large number of Senators against our very existence we can't afford to get mixed up in petty disturbances in the alcohol and tobacco field just to save a few dollars in taxes. Things like whiskey stills and marijuana patches should be handled by the local authorities."

"I know it should be Captain, but according to this report it seems that the local Sheriff could be a party to the illegal activities down there including possibly—even a murder."

The Captain looked at the Lieutenant and shook his head in disbelief. He stared thoughtfully at him for a moment. "Alright, Stewart, you take all six men and go check it out. Hell, they need to get out for a while anyway." The Captain got up and looked out the window from the top floor of the Federal building. "Stewart, where is this place. I'd like to know where you're going."

"It's at Smackover Captain. Just south of the corporate limits. It's beside a roadside beer joint called Mama's Place. The entire property is owned by a Maurine Muldoon. It's her two son's the Trooper said Blankenship told him was making the illegal whiskey." Looking out the window with his back to Lieutenant Stewart. The Lieutenant could not see the pale sickening gloom that assaulted Captain Vernon Stubbs face. His mind raced discomposedly through his secret times with Maurine. Times when she was but a young woman of loose morals, a slut. Times when he fought the thought that he may love her. The best of times in his life for sexual companionship. Times when he tried to no avail to change her way of life, which he eventually gave up on and just conceded to indulge himself occasionally in her amorous affection. Without turning around he addressed the Lieutenant. "Stewart, don't go down there arresting anyone. Just have the men destroy the marijuana patch. I'll be on down there about an hour behind you."

"Yes Sir." Lieutenant Stewart went out the door.

Vernon Stubbs at one time had been an undercover investigator for the FBI. When the government decided to make divisional fields of the ATF, he was transferred and promoted to Captain for the Arkansas field, headquartered in Little Rock. He was a stern and serious authoritarian, staunch and implacable. A dyed-in-the-wool disciplinarian.

Vernon stood six foot ten inches and hard as nails with exceptionally large feet. His foot ware was a size seventeen especially made for him. One morning in the hall at the Bureau, he overheard one of his men mention his Bureau nickname, which was only whispered in secrecy among the personnel. Ol'slewfoot will be here in a while, the man had said. It just happened that ol'slewfoot was right behind him. The man, a records coordinator, was fired on the spot for insubordination. An illustration of the Captains implacable discipline as an example to others.

Lieutenant Stewart and his six men dressed in full combat readiness with flack jackets, helmets and armed with high powered automatic assault weapons all rode together in an ATF Dingo, Duro 3 armored, mine protected transport and reconnaissance vehicle which could seat eight personnel and equipped with standard armament consisting of a remote controlled 7.62 mm machine gun turret and a 40 mm automatic grenade launcher. As promised, Captain Stubbs left one hour behind them driving his private car and in full field dress including his big heavy especially made combat boots, with a vastly impassioned feeling for Maurine ingrained deeply in his mind.

It was about mid-morning when the big Duro 3 pulled into the parking lot and continued on around to the side of the cornfield. Mama and Tommy Ray were talking out by Tommy Ray and Arlo's trailer when they saw it. "Wait a minute Mama." Tommy Ray said excitedly as he rushed into the trailer. He came out with Arlo's shotgun. "Here Mama, get this into the house, and hide it. I don't want Arlo gittin his self shot."

"Where is he?" asked Mama.

"He's in there sleepin', thank God. Ya'know how he's gona be."

Mama, holding Arlo's gun down to her side, hurriedly crossed the space from the trailer to the house and went through the back door. She came back out and met Tommy Ray near the back door. They watched the ATF commandos spread out along the cornfield and in unison start making their way into it as Lieutenant Stewart approached Mama and Tommy Ray. He pulled his helmet off. "Mam, are you Mrs. Maurine Muldoon?" he asked.

"No, no Mrs. Just plain Maurine. This here's my son, Tommy Ray, what th'fuck ya'll doin' on my property."

"Mam, we're from the Federal Bureau of Alcohol, Tobacco and Firearms. We have been authorized by our Captain to destroy a marijuana patch out there in your cornfield."

"A marijuana patch?" Mama acted surprised. "Now how the fuck do'ya spoze that could'of got into my cornfield?"

"I don't know mam, but we've got to destroy it if it's out there."

"Well yes, by all means, destroy it. I don't want nothing illegal on my property. It must'ta just come up naturally."

The men came out of the cornfield and gave the Lieutenant a positive sign, motioning to the center of the field. The Lieutenant told Mama he needed to commandeer the tractor and disc he noticed out by the sheds.

"I'll git'em fer'ya." Tommy Ray spoke up. "It's a trick'ta starting up the tractor." He left in a half run to go get the tractor and disc. He wanted to keep them as far away from his hothouse as possible. When he started the tractor, hooked up the disc and began driving it to the cornfield, the noise woke up Arlo. He came out of the trailer rubbing his eyes and walked up to where Mama and the Lieutenant were.

"What th'shitfire's goin' on out here with all the racket." he asked.

"They say there's a Goddamn marijuana patch in our cornfield." Mama said. "And they're gona destroy it."

The Lieutenant was watching Arlo's expression.

"What the fuck ya'know bout that." Arlo said, acting surprised. "Fuck it, I'm gona go back ta'bed." He sauntered back toward the trailer. The Lieutenant went out to the cornfield to direct the work of his men. Mama went and sat at the end table on the veranda where she could watch them work and prayed as best she knew how for the boys.

A car pulled up to the front of the building. Captain Vernon Stubbs got out, leaving his helmet in the car, and plodded up the steps onto the veranda. Mama quickly stood up as a rush of adrenaline overcame her. Not knowing whether to hug him or run, she said. "Well, kiss my fat ass. Vernon, you're one a'them."

"Guess so, Maurine. I'm their Captain. I've been thinking about you a lot, and wanting to see you, but not under these conditions."

Mama started to weep. She sit down and laid her head in her arms on the table. Vernon pulled a chair over next to her and sit down, consoling her.

"Maurine, what's this about a marijuana patch in your cornfield. Tell me about it."

Between sobs Mama told him it wasn't a patch. "It's only a few plants that the boys growed for their own use and they would never sell any. They knowed better than that. They are smart boys."

"What about the whiskey still?"

Mama raised up her head and looked at him. "Vernon, there is an old still out in the woods where my daddy made moonshine fer bout fifty years. He took care of all the poor people round Smackover. He raised me sellin' moonshine. It's an old run down still where the boys have always played. Them boys don't know doodlem shit bout makin' no moonshine. Even if'n they did they couldn't do it in that old dilapidated still. It hadn't been used in over forty years. Vernon, I'm gona tell'ya something bout them boys. I started many times ta'tell'ya afore, but figered the way I lived you wouldn't believe me. Well, here goes.—Vernon,—them two boys of mine are yer sons. I might'a been over sexed and slept round a lot, but one thing I do know. I know exactly who fathered all of my kids. I do hope it will have a bearin' on you goin' easy on'em bout the marijuana, but Vernon, that's not why I'm telling you bout'em. It's just something I've always wanted ta'do. And right now seemed like a good time."

Vernon, somewhat paled, stared at her for a considerable time before he bent over and kissed her on the cheek.

The tractor, pulling the disc had cut a big wide circle around the four plants and four stalks that had been harvested. The pieces of dead corn stalks that had been disced down and chopped up were raked up and piled on top of the so-called patch. The Lieutenant walked over to the end of the veranda and told the Captain he was going to set fire to the pile of chopped up cornstalks and burn up the marijuana patch.

"What ever, Stewart, but pull that tractor out of there first. You don't want it catching on fire."

Arlo had came back out. He and Tommy Ray was out front watching. Tommy Ray was acting nervous and prancing around unable to be still.

They both keep sneaking glances at the big man sitting with Mama. The six commandos and the Lieutenant stood out of the cornfield by the tractor watching the pile of dead cornstalks burn when all of a sudden.

KRAATHOOOOOMMUUMMMuummm....

The explosion shook the building, rotten limbs fell from the big tree in front of the Place. The commandos, the Lieutenant and the tractor were knocked over from the force of the blast as a great ball of fire shot straight up some seventy feet into the air somewhat akin to a baby atom bomb. The force from the blast also knocked over Mama and the Captain, as it did the boys. The Captain checked on Mama and then ran out to the field to see if his men were alright. Burning cornstalk debri and ashs sifted down for about twenty minutes. The remainder of the cornfield was laid over equally around the circumference of the gigantic hole in the ground.

"Lieutenant Stewart." Captain Stubbs said when he saw the Sheriff's car pull into the parking area maneuvering around the dead limbs. "You take the men and go back home while I try to figure out how the hell I'm going to explain to the local authorities why the ATF came down here and blew up someones damn cornfield.

And none of you are not to mention anything about it back at the office. By the time you get back there it better be completely forgotten. You understand."

When all had settled down, Vernon and Mama were left sitting on the veranda. "Maurine, those are good looking boys. I would like to get to know them. So, if you don't mind. I'll be coming back pretty regular." Mama stood up and planted a big smooch on his lips. "Ya'better be comin' back to git ta'know me too."

"Have you told them anything about me?"

"No, they've never asked about their father, so we've never talked bout it. I spoze they've thought bout it in their private moments, but they've never mentioned it."

"What do you think about us telling them. Do you reckon that will be alright?"

"I spoze so, Vernon. You want to do it now?"

Vernon, holding Mama's hand, Looked long and lovingly into her eyes as he thought about it. "No," he said. "Tell you what. I'll be back in about a week. You go ahead and tell them, and give it time to sink in. Then I'll spend some time with them when I return."

"Okay, Vernon. What ever you say." He kissed her again and left.

Mama, Tommy Ray and Arlo were in the kitch-
en when Tommy Ray told Mama the first partial
gallon that he hid was gone. "The disc must'a cut
the top of the plastic jug and the fuckin' fire got
to it." They stared at Tommy Ray momentarily
and burst into laughter. Mama was reflecting on
the proper way of telling them about their father.
She needed the right atmosphere. She was afraid
of their reaction if she just blurted it out.

"Ya'll know there's lot's of work to do in here
before we can open ta'night. There's dust all over
the tables and floor from that explosion. Arlo, go
tell the girls to come in here and start moping the
floor and cleaning the tables. Tommy Ray, you
get busy on the parking area. Git all the limbs
cleared up."

CHAPTER 11

Mama stepped up on the stage to an almost full house.

"Ladies and gentlemen. Welcome to another night of open mike at Mama's Place." she announced through the mike. "Looks like we have a goodly crowd. Do we have any entertainers?" A young man stood up from the nearest table. "Mama." he said. "There are three of us who would like to play and sing, if'n you'd give us a minute to get our equipment from the station wagon."

"Yes, please do. We would be delighted to hear'ya. What kind of music do'ya perform?"

"We do a variety of country songs. We'll be right back in." The three young men went out the door.

"Well now." Mama said to the audience. "This should be interesting. We hadn't yet had a trio."

Within minutes the young men entered. One had two guitars, an electric lead guitar and an acoustical with electric pick-ups. One had an electric base guitar and a black box with switches, dials and plug-ins on it. The other carried another mike and electrical wires. They went up on the stage and readily set it all up. There were now two mikes, a rhythm guitar, a lead guitar, a bass guitar and an electric drum set. They did a fast tuning up and adjusted the drum machine.

The young man with the rhythm guitar and the young man with the base guitar stepped up to the mikes. "Here's one of our own songs that everybody likes." the young man on the rhythm said. The music started and he began to sing a moderate country/folk style song. The crowd was absolutely mesmerized by the young mans articulate intonation. When he delivered the first high note in the chorus, "hereeee I go again," they went wild with enthusiastic applause but quickly stopped so as to hear the song. Couples began to dance between the tables dancing a moderately slow jitter-bug.

Others started pushing tables and chairs back out of the way.

"Like a run-away train…on
a downhill track… I'm
headin' for a crash…and
I can't turn back…

She's gona wreck my mind…
my head's in a spin…
she's gona break my heart…
here I go o-o-o… again…"

The two young men on the mikes beautifully harmonized the chorus as the lead guitarist picked
the melody.

"Hereeee… I go again…
don't think I'll ever win…
like the fool I've always
been…here I go o-o-o…
again…

Like hummin' birds nest…
in a honeysuckle vine…
she's made her bed…
right next to mine…"

They repeated the second verse and chorus.

"Like others I've loved…
no longer around…
she's keeping me home.
she's tyin' me down…"

All instruments joined in for a short instrumental piece including a harmonica played by the base player from a shoulder rest.

They again repeated the second verse, the chorus and the instrumental.

The crowd went absolutely ballistic, so to speak. They whistled, hollered and applauded for so long the trio could hardly get into their next number. When they did get started, they slowed the tempo and he sang another one of their own songs. A sad, contemporary tear-jerker.

> "Yes heart......
> I know you're sad
> and lonely...
> I'm afraid the hurting
> is here to stay...
> I drove away our reason
> for living...
> loneliness moved in...
> when she moved away...
>
> Lonely Heart......
> I'm sorry that I lost her...
> I'm sorry I never
> listen to you...

Lonely Heart......
I'm sorry that I cheated...
and I'm sorry
you belong to a fool...

Yes heart......
I hear your pain
and sorrow...
and it hurts to know
that she is gone...
the flames of love
no longer warm you...
now you must reap...
the misery I have sown...

lonely heart......
I know you're sad
and lonely...
I'm afraid the hurting
is here to stay...
I drove away our

reason for living...
loneliness moved in...
when she moved away...

yes heart......
I know that you
are crying...
I can feel the tears

like they were rain…
they chill my body
through and through…
if you're trying…
I guess you'll
drive me insane…"

They repeated the first chorus and ended with a short instrumental.

The people had shoved back tables and chairs to make room for dancing. Mama had Tommy Ray and Arlo to start stacking tables and chairs in the cove left in front of the old dance floor. Her wheels were turning again. She was amazed at how good these young men were and how the crowd took to them and wanted to dance to their music. She knew she couldn't let them get away. They were a gold mine. They continued to play and sing through the night. They covering songs by Hank Williams, Johnny Cash, Merle Haggard, George Jones, Merle Travis and others until Mama had to stop them on account of the mandatory closing time. No one had left. They all stayed, danced and bought lots of hamburgers and beer. The crowd wanted to know if they would be back tomorrow night. Mama asked them. Yes, they said they would. Mama announced it to the

crowd. Someone yelled, "Mama, you have time
for one more song."

"What do you think guys. Want ta'do one
more?"

"Sure" was the answer. The music started with a
swinging melody.

> "Let's all go down
> to Ludy's...
> let's all go have
> a ball...
> let's all go down
> to Ludy's...
> can you hear the
> ladies call...
>
> down at the end
> of Riverfront...
> the last house on
> the right...
> it's easy to find
> Ludy's place...
> just look for the
> red porch light...
>
> you'll find some
> lonely women...
> and painted ladies
> of the night...

down at the end
of Riverfront…
the last house on
the right…"

"Let's all go down
to Ludy's…
let's all go have
a ball…
let's all go down
to Ludy's…
can you hear the
ladies call…

Let's all go down
to Ludy's…
let's all go into town…
let's all go down
to Ludy's…
and lay our
money down …"

"Ludy is the greatest
madam…
in all of the river
towns…she knows
the needs of a man…
and she never lets
us down…

she'll call you a
lovely lady…
that leads a cheating
life…be careful what
you ask for…you might
just get your wife…"

They repeated the chorus twice.

How were they to know that Mama would especially like that song. She told them she had a great rendition of Red Wings they might like to learn. The one that seemed to be the leader said he believed he already knew it. But he's never found a place where he could sing it. "Yeah." Mama said. "That must be it."

Once the crowd had dispersed. Mama sit down with the three young men to see what it would take to keep them. "First of all." she said. "I know ya'll are not amateurs out playing open mike nightsso tell me what yer game is." The young man that played rhythm guitar and did the singing spoke up. "We put our act together while working on a dredge boat for a few years over on the Mississippi river. We played some real knock down, drag out honkytonks along the river towns. We wrote Ludy's about an actual brothel that we were told existed in Greenville way back in the forties. We have quite a few of our own songs but normally play what people are familiar with like songs from the top country stars. Now, what you want to hear is what our situation is. Well, we tried to get hooked up with a booking agent like you get you talent from for Saturday nights." He saw Mama's inquisitive look. "Oh yes, we did our homework before coming out here. You see, we are living in El Dorado. It is my home and these guys, my partners, Lewis and Clark, (he motioned to the other two) they are from over at Yazoo City in Mississippi. But are staying with me. By the way my name is Jonathon but I'm called Johnny. Johnny Sparrow. We call our trio simply Three Guys. Anyway, about the booking agent. They only book talent that performs for audiences. Our music is for dancing. So we are out looking for a job to play for people who dance. We want to get established, like in a honkytonk or country club or some place like yours. There you have it. We're just trying to survive and play our music."

"What are you guys ages?" asked Mama.

"We are all twenty-six." said Jonathon.

"If I cleared out these tables and chairs up front for a good size dance floor. How much money would it take to bring ya'll in here for say, four nights a week. That would be Tuesday through Friday. Monday is always a slow night.

I'm thinking bout just closing up on Monday. Ya'll talk it amongst yerself while I go in the back fer a minute. See if'n ya'want to make Mama's Place yer home. Oh, there'll be fringe benefits too. We have the best fuckin' hamburgers in the country. I'll git us all one started while I'm back there." Tommy Ray and Arlo were still in the back talking to Agnes and Arlene. "Have ya'll ate yet. I need four hamburgers and fries out front. Will ya'll make'em fer me. I might be gittin' them three guys fer full time. Keep yer fingers crossed." She went on into her bedroom. When she came out she told them to bring the hamburgers out to the table when they were ready and she went back out front "Guys, the burgers will be ready in a while. What have ya'll come up with?"

"Well, Mama." Jonathon said. 'We need to be working and we feel that anything right now is better than nothing. So if we could get three hundred dollars we might could make it on that."

"Jonathon, that sounds like a lot of money. What say let's clarify that somewhat. That's three hundred a night. Or three hundred each per night, or three hundred for the four nights, or three hundred each for four nights. Which is it?"

"Mam, what I meant was three hundred for all four nights that we would split up amongst us. That would a hundred dollars each."

"That sounds more like it but I had figured six hundred for all four nights which would give ya'll two hundred each. I wish I could afford more but right now the way I figure it. I'll be making bout the same as ya'll after all my expenses, but who knows, it could git better. We'll just have ta'see what happens. The one thing I do want ta'ask of you guys is. If I turn the Place into a honkytonk. I want'ya ta'stick with me and don't go leavin' me high and dry."

"Mama, if you want to have a contract made to that effect. We will be pleased to sign it. Want we guys."

"Yeah."

"Yeah, we sure will."

"Okay, you three guys. Here's my contract." She stuck out her hand for a handshake. They all vigorously shook her hand while smiling. "Oh." she said. "There is just one suggestion. Don't take umbrage to it. It's just a suggestion. I sure wish ya'll would do something bout that stupid name." Tommy Ray, Arlo and the girls brought the hamburgers out and Arlo asked them what they wanted to drink. Everyone said coke, even Mama. Mama told them that the band had joined the family and would be playin' regular and anytime they wanted a hamburger it was no charge. They were all happy and shook hands all around. Unbeknownst to anyone, Mama slipped Jonathon a hundred dollars. She allowed that they were probably broke. That was just the way with Mama.

"Mama, Mam." Lewis asked. "What do you think of The Backwoods Expedition?"

"Well, Lewis, I really don't know. I ain't never heard of 'em."

"No, I mean for a name. What do you think of The Backwoods Expedition for our name. When someone introduced us. It would fit with our names, Lewis and Clark. Like they could say, Let's give a big welcome to The Backwoods Expedition with Lewis and Clark. Featuring the incomparable Johnny Sparrow. Or they could just skip our names. It would still be a good name for us. What do you think?"

"Oh, yeah." Mama said enthusiastically. "I like it a lot. Yeah, that's good. That's real good, Lewis."

"You see guys." Lewis said. "I told you that's what we should call ourselves."

"Alright everybody." Jonathon said. "As of now we are officially called The Backwoods Expedition." Everyone gleefully acknowledged.

"I really like ya'lls singing." Arlo said. "Mama, bein's how, like you said, they've joined the family. Does that mean Agnes and Arlene have ta'give'em free pussy."

CHAPTER 12

Tommy Ray scooped out a hole in the potting soil, placed a plant in it and packed down the soil. He looked around at Mama. "Mama." he asked. "Do you put any credence in that there Charles Darwin's theory of evolution?"

"Where'd you hear bout that. I know they don't teach it in school."

"No, but our teacher once told us bout'em. He told it in such a way so's not ta'be teachin' his theory. What do you think bout it?"

"Bout what. Him, or his theory?"

"I knowed em." Arlo said. "I went ta'school with'em. He was a asshole."

Tommy Ray looked puzzled. "Who'er you talkin' bout, Arlo?"

"Bout Charles Darwins. I knowed him."

Mama was helping Tommy Ray and Arlo in the hothouse. They were transplanting some ten inch pot plants into bigger pots. They both looked questioningly at Arlo but did not comment. "Well," Mama answered. "I don't put no stock in his theory at all. We did not evolve from monkeys or apes or any other such animal. We were started out by Adam and Eve, who was made by God. So we are the children of God. Not of some Neo— Neapolitan man."

"That's Neanderthal Mama."

"Well, you know what I meant."

"How do'ya explain people that resemble apes or Neanderthals." Tommy Ray asked. "Do'ya reckon it's a throwback to their ancestral kind, like something in the genes. You remember there use ta'be a man walked around El Dorado all the time what looked like an ape. You remember, he walked kind'a bent over and his hands hung down ta'his knees. His head was even shaped like an ape. And what about the Bigfootswhere did they come from?"

"I don't know, Tommy Ray. Maybe there is some, what did ya'say, throwbacks? But it's damn well not us. We come from God. Maybe it's something' ta'do with the genes, like ya'said."

"Bullshit." Arlo said. "One of them Bigfeeted things couldn't even get into a pair of jeans. He couldn't get his feet through the legs."

"Tommy Ray, how many of these plants are ya'gona do." Mama asked. "I think ya'ought ta'put all the big pots in the end of the room and camouflage'em with something else. Something big and leafy, then put some tomato plants in front of that. We could save a lot of money with a bunch of good tomatoes. You could put the pots for the tomatoes all the way across bout three deep so's to make it hard to get to the back where yer weed is. I know, you could put bout three rows of climbing butter beans, with something for them to run on, between the weed and the tomatoes. That would hide yer pot fer sure."

"How the fuck would I get to'em. They have ta'be watered ya'know."

"Hell, Tommy Ray. Do I have ta'figure out everything fer'ya. You can find a fuckin' way ta'git ta'em." Mama figured she had avoided the inevitable long as she dared if she was going to make herself tell them. She mustered up the courage and blurted it out. "Did ya'll ever wonder who yer Daddy might be?"

"What brought that on, Mama?" Tommy Ray asked with astonishment.

"I use ta'think bout it some but finally just fergot bout it."

"Yeah, me too." Arlo said. "Do you know who he is?"

"If anybody does Arlo." Tommy Ray said. "It would be her, don't ya'think." Arlo looked exasperated at Tommy Ray. "I'll ask it again." he said. "Mama—do you know who he is?"

"Yes, I've always known. I just never thought it was a good idea ta'tell yall. I didn't want somebody ta'take yall away from me. I wanted yall all fer myself. Now, he knows he's yer father and wants to come and visit once in awhile to git ta'know yall better."

Tommy Ray and Arlo sit down on a couple of planting pots and looked ambiguously in disbelief at Mama for quite awhile. Arlo finally asked the important question. "Who is it?"

"Yall remember the big ATF man what was on the veranda with me when the cornfield blew up—we'll, that's him. His name's Vernon Stubbs. I been knowin' him fer years and years."

They stared at Mama for awhile before Arlo again spoke up. "Yeah, I saw ya'kiss'em. He's the man I saw you dancing with one night. Yall were dancing kind'a ugly—so I went ta'the trailer."

"I looked him over close that day he was here." Tommy Ray said. "And I was thinking that he was probably kin to the Bigfoot creatures. Having something ta'do with genetics. That's why I was asking you bout how the genes worked. I guess if we have some of his genes—that means we are probably kin to the Bigfoots."

Arlo stretched his legs out taking a good look at his feet. "I ain't got none'a his jeans." he said. "Shit—they'd swallow me."

"Vernon is not kin to no Bigfoot." Mama said. "He's a big man, and the Lord gave him big feet so's he could walk. Could you imagine him trying to walk on little feet. He would fall down. So, yall cut out the horseshit and be nice ta'him when he comes ta'visit. Damn'it, whether ya'like it or nothe's yer Daddy."

"We's kin ta'Angies bigfeeted baby." said Arlo.

"Yeah." Mama said. "But we don't carry the genes of Angies Bigfoot or her little one."

"Where's my shotgun at?" asked Arlo.

"I have it in my room. Tommy Ray brought it to me when the ATF showed up." said Mama.

"I figured as much." Arlo said. "I know I'm kinda slow sometimes but I'm not no fuckin' idiot. Ya'thought I'd go out there blastin away at them ATF's—didn't'ya T.R.—like I want'ta git myself kilt."

"No, Arlo." Tommy Ray said. "I don't think yer an idiot. I know ya'have plenty of sense. It's just that I know how sometimes you can git all highstrung."

"Mama." Arlo asked. "What the fuck is high-strung?"

"Alright now." Mama said. "Yall cut out the bullshit. We got things ta'do. I can hear the band in there rehearsing already. We're gona have a big night ta'night. We're gona have ta'contend with a room full of rowdy redneck men and women. Tommy Ray, you need ta'clean up and scrub yer-self real good. Then git in there and start gittin yer hamburger patties ready. Arlo, you git cleaned up too. I'm gona clean up and run over ta'see how Effie is faring. I won't be very long."

"Okay Mama." Tommy Ray said. "Tell'er hey fer me and Arlo."

"Yeah." Arlo said. "When's she gona have that baby?"

"Bout another four or five weeks, Arlo."

"Well. tell'er ta'hurry it up."

By the time Mama returned, couples had began to come in and take seats around the dance floor. The young men in the band were sitting in the kitchen having a coke and talking with Tommy Ray, Arlo, Agnes and Arlene. Someone had made a funny and they were laughing when Mama came in. "Did I miss a good one?" she asked.

"Arlo was telling us bout a Bigfoot tryin' to wear a pair of jeans." Clark said. "But he couldn't git his feet through the legs."

"Yeah." Mama said. "That Arlo is a real card sometimes. It's bout ten minutes till eight. We might as well git started. There's a lot of rowdy rednecks out there."

"Okay guys." Jonathan said. "Let's do it."

"Let me go up first." Mama said. "I want ta'introduce'ya. Yall come on up while I'm doin' it." She went out first, picked up a note from under the edge of the cash register and went up on the stage. She tapped on the mike to see if it was on. It was. "Ladies and Gentlemen" she announced. "I want to extend a hearty Redneck welcome ta'all of yall. The crowd had quieted down. Mama looked at her note. "Now, let's all give a big Mama's Place welcome to (she raised her voice) The Backwoods Expedition, with Lewis and Clark (she motioned to them as they put their guitar straps over their heads) and featuring the incomparable (she motioned to him and again raised her voice) Johnny Sparrow." She stepped off the stage and sit on her barstool. "Thank you, Mama." Johnny said. And they went right into Hank Williams, Jambalaya. The people hit the floor jitter-bugging. They followed that with two more Hank Williams songs. "If You've Got The Money, I've Got The Time" and "I'm So Lonesome I Could Cry."

"Alright now. How we doin' out there. Is everybody havin' fun." The crowd whistled, hollered and applauded. "We're now gona do a little slow rock-a-billy thing from Jim Feazell, called This Time—Auh-one—auh-two" The music started and Johnny sang.

"She thinks I'll send her
pretty flowers…
and a card begging her…
honey please…
but I think I'll wreck her
ivory towers…
and let her crawl back on
her knees…

we've played this same old
game before…
with no rhyme or reason…
I can see…
she screams goodbye and
slams the door…
and leaves the making up
all to me…

This time......
there's gona be some
changes made...
I'll not give in...
I'll not pretend...

This time......
there's gona be some
changes made...
no crying her name..
no playing her game...

she thinks I'll send her
pretty flowers...
and rain down on her...
loving kisses...
but I think I'll wait a few
more hours...
and see if there's
something she misses...

no more will I confess
my sorrow...
for things I know are just
not true...maybe I'll let
her worry until tomorrow...
wondering where I am and
what to do...

This time......
there's gona be some
changes made…
I'll not give in…
I'll not pretend…

This time…
there's gona be some
changes made…
no crying her name..
no playing her game..

They then went right into another Jim Feazell song. "I'm Patchin Up An Old Love Affair." followed by Johnny Cash's "Guess Things Happen That Way." and "Ring Of Fire". The night flew by extremely well with songs made famous by Marty Robbins, Merle Haggard and others.

The next two nights were no different. They played and sang to a packed house each night. Friday night had came quick. The night that would finish their first week. Everyone was ecstatic with the way things had gone. They all were looking forward to Saturday and the performance of Marie Lebeaux. The boys in the band had asked Mama if they could come in and hear her. Certainly, she had said. They did not realize that Marie Lebeaux would be here tonight listening to them. She had performed the previous night in Hot Springs, spent the night, and drove down here. Her intentions were to see just what kind of place she would be working, but decided since it was almost eight o'clock, she would stay and hear the band. She sat alone at a small table near the end of the bar and ordered a hamburger and a beer.

CHAPTER 13

The Backwoods Expedition was introduced in
the same manner as the three preceding nights.
Mama's Place was again packed. Johnny went
right into a bright up-beat Jim Feazell country/
folk song entitled, "Louisiana River Boat Man."
in an open key of "D". The floor filled for an easy
paced jitterbug.

> "Ain't nothing better in
> this life for me...
> than living on the river
> and being free...
> I go when I want
> and I do what I please...
> I sit on my deck in the
> evening breeze...

I've been everywhere that
a boat can go...there's not
a river that I don't know...
I brew my coffee in the late
afternoon.. and do a little
fishing by the light of
the moon...

Lewis harmonized the chorus with Johnny.

I'm a Louisiana...
river boat man...
my blood's made of
muddy water and sand...
I've got a gal in every
town I know...all the way up
to the big Ohio... all the way
up to the big Ohio...

some folks, they call me a
river rat...but I don't care
cause I like it like that...
I wouldn't trade my life for
any in the world...cause I'm
happy with my boat and a
river town girl...

I go into town every
Saturday night...sometimes
I gamble...sometimes I fight.

but one thing you can bet as
sure as you're born…I'll be
back on the river come
Sunday morn…"

They repeated the chorus.

"We're pleased to see all of you good people
here tonight." Johnny announced as the danc-
ers returned to their seats. We're going to slow
the tempo now and give all you guys that like
to dance up close and slow, a real treat with another Jim Feazell classic—"You're A Lady." Clark
picked a short introduction and Johnny began to
sing soft, slow and heavyhearted.

"I saw you and you're new
love today.. from where I sit..
I heard him loud and clear…
my heart sank when he called
you baby.. and on your cheek..
I thought I saw a tear…

before you break my heart
into…there's something I
want to say to you…
a gentleman never calls a
lady… baby……doesn't
he know… you're… a…
lady…"

"The first time I saw you
smile.. and the first time
we talked awhile.. the
first time I kissed your
hand… and the first time
I was… your man…
I knew…that you…
were a lady…"

"will he love you more
than life itself… will his
pedestal be as high as
mine…will he ever learn
to be.. respectful.. and
will he worship you all
the time…

before you tear my world
apart.. take a good look
into his heart…
a gentleman never calls a
lady…… baby… doesn't
he know… you're…. a….
lady…"

"The first time I saw you
smile…and the first time
we talked awhile… the
first time I kissed your

hand… and the first time…
I was your man… I knew…
that you… were a lady…

Except for two Hank Williams songs. The Backwoods Expedition was featuring Jim Feazell songs for the first half of the set. They went on to do "Dance With Me." / "Coffee Shop Show." / "Patchin' Up An Old Love Affair." / "No One's To Blame." / "Let Me Be Lonely." and "I Had A Feelin'." They closed out the first half of the night, before the break, with the Jim Feazell classic "Walk Away." a moderately up beat song in the key of "D". Clark gave it a short 1/2 stanza intro. Johnny sang.

> "The band was playing a
> honkytonk song…the room
> was swaying.. to love gone
> wrong…my friend was
> making.. time with my baby..
> and I heard her say….
> walk away…..
>
> Walk away……
> that's what she said…
> I'll walk away…
> with you tonight…
> Walk away……

I heard her say…
I'll walk away…
it'll be alright…

we were all drinking…
more than our share.. my
baby was talking… like
I wasn't there…she
must'ta been thinking…
I didn't care..
and I heard her say……
walk away……

Walk away……
that's what she said…
I'll walk away…
I love you so…
Walk away…
I heard her say…
I'll walk away…
he'll never know…

my baby was crying…
down my forty-four…
my friend was trying..
to get out the door..
I busted his head.. and
shot my baby dead…
and I heard her say……

walk away…..

Walk away……
that's what she said…
I'll walk away…
with you tonight…

Walk away……
I heard her say…
I'll walk away…
it'll be alright…
Walk away……
that's what she said…
I'll walk away…
I love you so…

Walk away……
I heard her say…
I'll walk away…
he'll never know…

As Johnny ended the song. Clark announced a break. "We'll be back in fifteen." he said. He and Lewis laid their guitars on the floor at the back of the stage and headed for the restroom. Jonathon had been noticing the pretty young woman at the small table near the end of the bar. He knew she was alone and not dancing with anyone. He made his way to her table to, as he thought, *"check her out"*. He pulled up a chair and asked permission, unlike normal redneck etiquette, to set down. "Sure." she said with a smile. "Please do." He sat down. "Are you enjoying the music." he asked. "I couldn't help but notice that you are alone." My name is Johnny Sparrow." He extended his hand. "Yes I know." she said as she took his fingers and lightly shook. "I have marveled at your singing. You're very good Johnny, my name is Marie Lebeaux. I'll be performing here tomorrow night. Johnny arose partially almost jumping out of his seat. "Miss Lebeaux." he exclaimed. "I had no idea it was you. Sorry,—I meant to say—that you was she. I had no idea. "You're early. Wha—let me start over. I'm pleased to meet you, Miss Lebeaux.

"I'm pleased to meet you too, Mister Sparrow. She smiled big and bewitchingly. "Please call me Marie." Marie Lebeaux was not what one might call beautiful, but yet charmingly attractive. Her long shinny black hair hung loosely down her back. Her eyes were an enticing light green and her teeth seemed overly white due to her natural complexion of appearing to be heavily tanned. She had a nice figure, not foxy or statuesque, but nice and pleasing. Johnny got over his initial shock and the fifteen minutes went by fast. Among other tidbits she told him she was normally referred to as the Cajun nightingale. He asked her if she would stay so they could talk more. She said she would.

Now, Melissa Marie Lebeaux should not be confused with, or thought to be a decedent of the well renowned Marie Laveau, Voodoo queen of New Orleans who passed away in 1881 at the age of 98. Even though she did leave a great multiplicity of hereditary descent in bearing fifteen children.

To accentuate the validity of the voodoo lady named Marie Laveau. An accomplished singer/songwriter who makes teddy bears named after him wrote a great song about her. If you didn't leave her alone, it said. She'd go "Grrrooukaa" another man done gone. No, our Marie Lebeaux doesn't growl. She sings as sweetly as a Cajun nightingale.

CHAPTER 14

The band opened the second half with another Jim Feazell song. A bright, moderately fast, country stomp called "Hurtin' All Over". The jitter-buggers hit the floor in full force as Johnny sang.

"Well maybe I lie… but
baby I try…and I can't
help it when I cry…cause
you got me……
hurtin' all over…
hurtin' all over…
waitin' achein'
anticipatin'…your lovin'.

come on baby… be mine…
don't keep me on the line…
I'd cross the burnin' desert
sand…just to be your
lovin'man…"

"Well maybe I lie… but
baby I try…and I can't
help it when I cry…cause
you got me……
hurtin' all over…
hurtin' all over…
waitin' achein'
anticipatin'… your lovin'.

come on baby… be good…
do like you know you
should…I'd swim the
deepest ocean blue…
just to lay down
beside you…"

come on baby… be true…
I'd trade my kingdom for
you…I'd give the moon
and stars above…
just for a night
of your love…"

"Well maybe I lie…but
baby I try…and I can't
help it when I cry…
cause you got me……
hurtin' all over…
hurtin' all over…
waitin' achein'
anticipatin'…your lovin'."

As soon as Hurtin' All Over ended Clark picked the famous chicki boom chicki, freight train rhythm trademark sound of Johnny Cash. Made famous by his lead guitarist, Luther Perkins. Everyone thought Johnny Sparrow was going to sing.

The music abruptly stopped and Johnny asked. "How many of yall know what possessed Johnny Cash to write Ring Of Fire?" No one spoke up. He said. "Well, he reached for the Preparation H. And got the Ben Gay instead. Clark, on the lead guitar gave a fan fair sounding like scratchy laughter.

"SCRRR.. RATTTTCHEEE.. HEEEE".

That bit of humor brought the house down and they then continued to play, sing and watch the people dance to numerous old standards for the next hour. Johnny looked at the clock. It was ten minutes until the witching hour. "Alright friends". he said. "It's getting close to time to go to Ludy's". They had closed ever night with the Ludy's chorus. "But before we do, I want to sing you a short little diddy that's always been a favorite of my, because it stretches and exercises the vocal chords. It's entitled, I Love You So Much It Hurts Me—or Who Put The Sand In The Vaseline."

"I love you… sooooo
much… it hurts me…
and there's nothingggg…
I can dooooo…I want to
hold you my dearrrrr….
for ever and ever……
I love you sooooo much…
it hurrrttttss……
meeeee….. soooooooo."

"Let's all go down
to Ludy's…
let's all go have
a ball…

let's all go down
to Ludy's…
can you hear the
ladies call…

Let's all go down
to Ludy's…
lets all go into town…
let's all go down
to Ludy's…
and lay our
money down…"

"Everybody drive carefully and don't for-
get nine o'clock tomorrow night. It will be the
Queen of song. The melodious bird of paradise.
The incomparable Cajun Nightingale. Miss MA-
RIE LEBEAUX."

Arlo dimmed the stage lights. The people
were filing out and Jonathon went back to the
table with Miss Lebeaux.

Mama had noticed the young lady by herself
and how she was enjoying listening to Johnny,
and seeing him spend his break with her. Mama
don't ever stay in the dark for long. She's never
been nobody's fool, as she says. The introduction
as the Cajun nightingale did it. She knew this
had to be Marie Lebeaux. She had not heard that
term and knew that neither had Johnny. She sat
on her stool and watched them, wondering if she
was going to be introduced. If not, she was damn
well going to butt in.

As the last of the customers went out, Jonathon and Marie got up and approached Mama. "Mama". Jonathon said. "Let me introduce Marie Lebeaux." Mama got off the stool and extended her hand. "I'm very pleased to meet you, Miss Lebeaux." she said as Marie shook her hand. "Yer runnin' kind'a early—ain't'cha."

"Please call me, Marie." she said. "Yes, I guess I am, but it's for a reason, I needed to see your club and talk to you before tomorrow." Mama looked in wonderment at her. "Tell'ya what." Mama said. "Let's go to the kitchen and talk. I need some coffee."

"Sounds good to me." Marie said. "I would like some too."

"Arlo, go put on a pot of coffee." Mama said as she put all of the folding money from the cash register into a bank bag. She took the bag with her as they all followed Arlo into the kitchen. Tommy Ray had anticipated them coming into the kitchen and had the table cleared. Agnes and Arlene were making hamburgers for themselves and the band. Mama introduced everyone to Marie as they sit down at the table.

"You really a Cajun?" asked Arlo.

"Yes." Marie chuckled lightly. "That's what they tell me."

"Pay no attention to Arlo." Mama said. "He's sometime rude. But he means well. We'll be gittin' the Place all cleaned up in the morning, and the tables and chairs back onto the dance floor fer'ya. Ya'say you needed ta'talk bout something?"

"Yes, first of all, let me ask you if you have talked to the booking agency."

"As a matter of fact." Mama said. "I've been trying to reach Mister Green. It seems I can never git past a secretary. They have not sent me any information on my next performer after you. I needed it before now so's to start some promotion."

"Mama." Marie said. "They called me yesterday at my hotel in Hot Springs. They told me to come down here today and check out your operation, and see if I wanted to perform here—or not. They left it up to me." Mama looked expressionless at her. Everyone else had stopped what they were doing and listened. "I guess they were to chicken-shit to tell you." Marie said. "They left it up to me. Mama, they're not going to book anyone else in here. They said you misrepresented yourself in telling them you operated a private comedy and social club. When in reality, they said they found out, is nothing but a rough and rowdy liquor drinking night club, or as Mister Green said. A damn redneck honkytonk."

There was silence all around. "I think that coffee is done, Arlo." Marie said. "It sure smells good. Could I have some?" Arlo poured a cup of coffee and put it on the table for her. She took a sip and said. "Mama, I'll call him and explain the situation. I don't know if it will help. But I'll try."

"No, just let it drop." Mama said. "If he didn't have the decency ta'call me his'self. I don't think I need to deal with him. We'll git along just fine. So what do you think Marie, are you go'na perform. There's a lot'ta folks lookin' forward to hearin' you. You want some sugar and milk fer your coffee?"

"Mama, you forget. I'm a Cajun. We all drink our coffee black and strong, and yes Mam, I certainly do want to sing. I'm sure all will be well in your club. Mama, before I hooked up with the booking agency, I free lanced all over south Louisiana, and let me tell you, you've never seen the like of rowdiness until you work a redneck Cajun honkeytonk. So, don't you worry Mama, I'll be just fine."

"What kind of songs do you sing?" asked Lewis.

"Well, foremost, I'm considered a folk singer, but I do deviate from that somewhat. I will usually open with a couple of blues numbers from the legendary Bessie Smith from the twenties and thirties. Like Jealous Blues and Nobody Knows You When You're Down And Out. Then I'll definitely do some early Joan Baez, the undisputed Godmother of folk. I especially like Lonesome Road, I Once Loved A Boy, Fifteen Months, and Angeline. I'll also do some Joni Mitchell, and a few others. Then I always close with Oh, I forgot, I'll have two or three of my own mixed in there somewhere. I might even do a Bob Dylan or two. I especially like I'll Be Your Baby Tonight. And then there's some old favorites like House Of The Rising Sun and Midnight Special."

Marie finished her coffee, told everyone how pleased she was to have met them and said she must get on to the motel and get some rest. "I'll see yall tomorrow evening. Jonathon will you walk me out to the car?"

"I'll have ta'unlock the door fer'ya." said Arlo.

"Thanks Arlo.—Clark, walk out with us for a minute."

Out by the car, Marie turned to Clark. "Clark, I'm going to take Johnny with me so I don't get lost. You and Lewis just go on home and don't worry about him. We have a lot of talking to do." Clark went back in and Arlo locked the door. "He's gona go fuck'er, ain't he."

"I doubt that Arlo." said Clark.

"Ha, I bet'cha he is."

Marie pulled out onto the highway and headed toward El Dorado.

"Johnny, you don't mind me calling you Johnny, do you."

"Of course not. I'd rather you did."

"Well, Johnny, you probably don't realize what it's like being on the road all the time. It's impossible to have a steady boyfriend, and it's only very occasionally I run up on someone that I really like. Someone I feel safe about going to bed with. And guess what Johnny. You've grabbed the golden ring. The first time in about six months. I told Clark for him and Lewis to just go on home. There's no objections from you, are there. I'm extremely horny." Johnny, with a tinge of anxiousness rubbed his sweaty palms and thought, *Dear God, what have I done to deserve such a blessing.* "No, no objections, on the contrary I'm delighted and grateful that it was I who grabbed the ring."

"AHEEEE AHHHH" yelled Marie. Johnny was momentarily alarmed until he saw her jubilant expression. She had just exclaimed a sound of joy known in south Louisiana as the Cajun yell.

He directed her to the Holiday Inn where she had called her reservation in from the hotel in Hot Springs. Within a matter of minutes they were in the room and getting to know one another quite completely.

CHAPTER 15

Mama stepped up to the mike. "Ladies and Gentlemen." she said enthusiastically. Mama's Place takes great pleasure in presenting for your listening pleasure. The incomparable Cajun nightingale. Miss Marie Lebreaux. Let's give her a big Mama's Place welcome." Marie went up on the stage, picked her guitar up from against the back wall and put the strap over her head. She sported a big blond six string acoustical Guild with electric pick-up. She plugged it in to the mixer. It had been plugged in and balanced earlier. She stepped up to the mike as Mama went and sit on her stool.

"Hello." Marie said with a big smile. "Most of you probably never heard of Bessie Smith. She was the Mother of blues, back in the 20's and 30's.

To get things started I'm going to sing you an old Bessie Smith blues number called Gimme A Pigfoot." She did a guitar intro with string bending blues effects. Marie could almost make her guitar talk. She began to play a bluesy jazz rhythm in the key of D with the 3rd and 7th flatted optionally. She sang, accentuating and enunciating each syllable to perfection. Her harmonious voice was rich and sweet to the ear. The audience was as quiet as a church mouse. Not a sound uttered. Everyone loved good music, especially erudite rednecks, and as far as music appreciation went, they were in the presence of excellence.

The audience stood and applauded as Marie hung her guitar down to her side and graciously bowed repeatedly. They did not sit down until Marie raised her guitar up and stepped up to the mike strumming a folk melody. She sang a sad song called San Francisco Mable Joy. Written by Joan Baez, the undisputed Godmother of modern folk. That was followed by a few other early Joan Baez songs written before she went politically, so to speak, and began writing protest songs. She sang Lonesome Road, I once Loved A Boy, Fifteen Months and Angeline. When she sang San Francisco Mable Joy, if anyone had looked they could have seen Mama wiping tears from her eyes. She sang a couple Joni Mitchell songs,

Come To The Sunshine and The Way It Is. "For those of you who are not familiar with the song Midnight Special" she said. "I'll tell you a quick story about it so you will understand what it is about. A long time ago, about halfway between Houston and Dallas was a State Penitentiary. The Midnight Special was a passenger train that ran the route back and forth between the two cities. Every night about midnight the train passed the prison with it's big headlight swinging from one side to the other across the track. As it passed the prison the light would fall on the prison wall a couple of times before it got by. Now, being holed up in a state pen, one would put faith in most anything that would give him a glimmer of hope. It was said by the inmates that if the light shined on you, you would be set free. So, they all climbed up to their small windows when it was time for the Midnight Special to come streaking by blowing it's whistle and swinging it's light. They all prayed for the light to shine on them." She sang.

> "If you ever go to Houston…
> boy you better walk right…
> you better not stagger…
> and you better not fight…

Sheriff Benson will arrest
you…and he'll surely sit
you down…if the Judge
finds you guilty…boy
you're penitentiary bound"

"Let the Midnight Special…
shine her light on me…
Let the Midnight Special…
shine her ever-loving light
on me…"

we'll, you wake up in the
morning… you hear the
ding-dong ring…you go
a'marching to the table,
you see the same
damn thing…

hard biscuits on the table…
cold grits in the pan…
you say a thing about it…
you're in trouble with
the man"

"Let the Midnight Special…
shine her light on me…
Let the Midnight Special…
shine her ever-loving light
on me…"

yonder comes Miss Rosie…
how in the hell do you
know…I can tell by the
apron…and the dress
she wore…

umbrella on her shoulder…
piece of paper in her hand
she's going to the warden…
to tell him turn loose
her man…"

"Let the Midnight Special…
shine her light on me…
Let the Midnight Special…
shine her ever-loving light
on me…

"Let the Midnight Special…
shine her ever-loving light
on me…"

She repeated it one more timeup tempo.

"Let the Midnight Special…
shine her ever-loving light
on me….. Whooo Yeahll."

After the applause had ended, she announced that she was going to try one of her own songs on them. "I call it That's The Chance, I hope you

like it." It was a soft strumming accompaniment.
She sang

"Listen to the sound of a
far away train…hear the
cry of a mournin' dove…
taste the sweetness of an
April rain…know the
warmth of a woman in
love…

another summer's coming
on…another heart will
have to break…by early
morning he'll be gone…
but that's the chance I
said I'd take…"

"Bet your dreams on a
wandering heart…take a
chance love will grow…
kiss away tears when
lovers part…take
another chance on a
restless soul…"

listen to the call of geese
in flight…hear the sound
of falling leaves…feel
the breeze of an autumn

night…know the hurt of
a heart that grieves…

another winter's coming
on…another heart will
have to break…by early
morning I'll be gone…
but that's the chance he
said she'd take.."

"Bet your dreams on a
wandering heart… take
a chance love will grow…
kiss away tears when
lovers part…take
another chance on a
restless soul…"

listen to the silence of
love grown cold…see
the writing on the wall…
search for reasons never
told…have the strength
to take the fall…

another spring is coming
on…another heart will
have to break…by early
morning he'll be gone…
but that's the chance

I said I'd take…

"Bet your dreams on a
wandering heart…take a
chance love will grow…
kiss away tears when
lovers part…take
another chance on a
restless soul…"

Another standing ovation for the Cajun nightingale.

Marie had gone past her two hour performance time. She thanked the audience and
praised them for being so good, leaned her guitar
against the back wall and went into the kitchen.
The audience continued to applaud, whistle and
chant "more" for a good five minutes before Marie returned to the stage. She put her guitar strap
back over her head and stepped up to the mike.
"Thank you—thank you." she said and began to
sing,

"Put your hand in the
hand of the man who
stilled the water…put
your hand in the hand
of the man who calmed
the sea…take a look at

yourself and you can
look at others
differently...by putting
your hand in the hand
of the man from Galilee...

Every time I look into
the holy book I want to
tremble...when I read
about the part where a
carpenter cleared the
temple...for the buyers
and the sellers were no
different fellers than
what I profess to be...
and it causes me pain
to know that I'm not the
gal that I should be...

Mama taught me how to
pray before I reached the
age of seven...and when
I'm down on my knees
that's when I'm close to
heaven... Daddy lived his
life with two kids and a
wife...you do what you
must do...but he showed
me enough of what it

takes to get you through…

Put your hand in the
hand of the man who
stilled the water…put
your hand in the hand
of the man who calmed
the sea…take a look at
yourself and you can
look at others
differently…by putting
your hand in the hand
of the man from Galilee…

Put your hand in the
hand of the man
from Galilee……"

Marie again thanked the audience as she was getting a standing ovation. She again put her guitar by the back wall and waved at the people as she went into the kitchen. Mama went onto the stage and told the people it was a few minutes past closing time and that was it for the night. Arlo dimmed the stage lights and raised the house lights. Marie came out to the bar and signed autographs for about fifteen minutes before all the people left.

Mama hugged Marie and almost cried telling her how much she enjoyed her performance. "Mama." Marie said. "I'm going to call Mister Green and tell him the mistake he's making. I've never played to a better audience."

"That's cause they've never heard anyone near good as you. I'd just as soon let it drop. I'll get along fine just runnin' a honkytonk."

CHAPTER 16

Back at the Holliday Inn for a final farewell. Marie said. "Johnny, you must know you and the boys are much to good to be wasting your talent here. It's now that you need to be making some headway on your careers."

"Your better than us. And you're still playing bookings around the country." he said.

"Johnny, I have a recording contract from Capital Records and I just tonight did my last booking for the agency. When I leave here this morning, I go straight to Thibodaux for a couple of days and then fly to L.A. They say they are arranging performances for me at folk clubs and coffee houses so I can work some while I'm recording. They say I'll be recording about everything I know for future albums."

"How did you get all that set up?"

"What you've got to do is quit spinning your wheels. You'll always be in the same rut. Go find a decent recording studio. There is probably one right here in El Dorado. Make some good demo tapes of your own songs and start sending them out to record labels. Let them know what you're doing and that you're looking for a recording contract. We'll stay in touch, and when you get one made, send me a copy and I'll see that they listen to it at Capital. Be sure to give me your Mothers address before I take you home."

Marie got out of the bed and went to the shower. While the water ran, Jonathon wrestled with his conscious about the promise he made to Mama. He thought, *"What the hell, it certainly want hurt nothing to make some demos. They might not like us anyway."* His thoughts were cut short as the water stopped. He had not even attempted to get out of bed, but it made no difference, she came out of the bathroom and jumped back in bed with him. It seemed that she was going to get a late start to Thibodaux.

As time had fast slipped into mid-summer. Effie was at home nursing a fine baby redneck. He looked just like his daddy. The band was working five nights a week, Tuesday through Saturday, and having a full house every week. Mama was more than pleased to be operating a full fledged honkytonk.

Another Saturday evening, the band was on stage getting ready to start the last night of the week. Mama, the boys and all the help were sitting at tables near the bar having a cola. They had about an hour before opening.

"Any of ya'll want to sing a song to warm us up." Johnny asked.

"Yeah." Tommy Ray said. "I'll sing a little one."

"Shit." said Arlo. "You can't sing."

"Come on up here." Johnny said. "What'cha gona' sing?"

Tommy Ray took a mike and held it. "It's just a little thing I like ta'sing."

"You go ahead T.R.—we'll follow you.

"Okay, he said—and he sang.

> "I'm lookin' under..
> the skirts of Wanda..
> that I've looked under
> before…
>
> first are the ankles…
> the second the knees…
> third are the panties…

that blow in the breeze…

there's no need
explaining…the one
remaining…it's
something that I adore…

I'm lookin' under..
the skirts of Wanda..
that I've looked under
before…"

Johnny had picked up on his melody quickly and kind of followed him. They all applauded him. Except Arlo.

"Shit." said Arlo. "I can beat that all ta'hell."

"Well, git yer ass up there and do it." Tommy Ray said sarcastically.

Arlo went on stage and took the mike. "Can ya'play My Bonnie Lies Over The Ocean. In the key of G." he said. As he looked pugnaciously at Tommy Ray.

"Sure, let's do it boys." They started playing and Arlo sang.

"My Bonnie lies over
the ocean…
my Bonnie lies over
the sea…

my Bonnie lies over
the ocean
don't bring my Bonnie
back to me…

my Bonnie has
tuberculosis…
my Bonnie has
one rotten lung…
she spits up the
bloody corruption…
and rolls it around
on her tongue…

leave'er there…
leave'er there…
don't bring my
Bonnie to me…
leave'er there…
leave'er there…
leave my Bonnie
across the sea."

Everyone looked at Arlo in absolute amaze-
ment as he replaced the mike and took his seat.
They were totally flabbergasted.

"God'damn, Arlo." Tommy Ray said. "That
was fuckin' sick."

Over near the front door, Vernon Stubbs had came in unnoticed and was seated in a chair. Everyone was startled as he laughed loudly and applauded.

"Good job, boy—good job!" he bellowed.

Mama immediately got up and went over to Vernon. They sat and talked quietly. Most of the others went to the kitchen, including the two new girls that Mama had hired as waitresses. They had worked out real well. Arlo was attracted to one of them, but it had only gotten to a courting stage.

Mama went into the kitchen to see Arlo. It was almost time to open. She asked Arlo to take over for her. To introduce the band and handle the cash register. She told him she was going to her room with his Dad to discuss some important business.

"Sure" he said with a sly smile. "It must really be important fer'ya ta'not be in the club."

"You just do like yer asked."

"You go on and don't worry bout it, Mama. I can handle it."

Mama went out and got Vernon. They came back through the kitchen and to her bedroom. The four girls, Arlo, Tommy Ray and a couple of band members watched them go into Mama's bedroom. They heard the door lock. They all looked at each other.

"That's my Dad." Arlo said. "He's got some Bigfeets jeans. But he can put'em on. His feets ain't as big as my brother in-laws. They all looked bewilderedly at Arlo—even Tommy Ray.

All went well for the night. Mama wasn't even missed. But Arlo said not to tell her that.

Sunday morning at the breakfast table in the kitchen. Mama told the boys that their Dad had some important news to tell them. Vernon took a sip of coffee and looked at them.

"Well" he said. "What it amounts to is that I'm only going to get to stay a couple of days, for right now. I really hate that. I wanted to spend a lot of time with you—What happened was, I heard from my aunt up in Washington state. She told me my Mother, your Grandmother, was worsening. She said she had Alzheimer's disease. I have to go see her before she completely loses her faculties." Tommy Ray and Arlo had stopped eating and was listening intently to him. He took a bite of scrambled eggs, a sip of coffee and looked at them.

"Tell'em the rest of it." Mama said. "We were talking bout just that very thing out in the hothouse a while back."

"Well, yeah." Vernon said hesitantly. "Well, you see, where I was raised in a little mountain town up there in Washington. It is known to be Sasquatch or Bigfoot country. They live all up in them mountains. And, well—I have reason to believe I may carry Bigfoot genes.—That's why I have got to talk to my Mother while she might still remember some things."

"Gol-lee" Arlo said. "Cause yer big and have big feets. Ya'think that cause yer feets are hard to git through yer jeans?"

Vernon looked at Arlo inquisitively. "Yeah, something like that." Then he looked at Mama. "You know, Maurine, I like that boy."

"Yeah" she said. "He's got a head on'em."

"That's fer sure." said Tommy Ray.

"I thank God, Maurine, that no hereditary Bigfoot characteristics showed up in the boys. On account of my suspicions of having the genes, I did some studying up on the subject. It seems that the reproduction of unrelated genes from an ancestral carrier may be nonexistent for years, or then on the other hand it could at any time reproduce partially or completely the hereditary features of the existing gene."

"That's what we was referring to as a throwback." said Tommy Ray as he looked at Mama. She nodded her head.

"Yes" Vernon said. "That's exactly what it would be. A throwback of the ancestral gene.—I took an extended leave of absence from my job. I'm going to stay here for a couple of days and then go back to Little Rock and get a flight home. When I get back, I'm thinking of just retiring."

"Well" Arlo said. "Dad, you tell Grandma hey fer me. And tell'er I hope that ol'timers disease don't hurt much."

"Okay Arlo, I'll be sure to tell her.—Tommy Ray, finish your breakfast and let's go look at your pot. Your Mama said you were going to have trouble watering it. Maybe I can help you figure it out."

Tommy Ray paled when he looked at Mama. She smiled at him. He started eating fast. "Yeah, okay." he said.

Vernon looked the situation over in the hothouse. He told Tommy Ray to make him a crawl space around the other end of the butter beans, so he could get to the plants to cultivate them. And take the water hose he saw out by the trailer and run it up the end of the hothouse securing it to the outside two-by-four and tie it inside along the rafter for about three feet. Put a sprinkler on the end of it. Then all he'd have to do is turn the water on to water the plants.

Tommy Ray smiled, thanked him and said he would get right to it.

Vernon spent that day and the next getting to know the boys. He liked them immensely and hoped to return soon. It made him feel good to be a father. He knew it would not be long until Tommy Ray too, would call him Dad. Arlo asked Tommy Ray to get out some of the weed he had saved from the cornfield. Tommy Ray reluctantly broke it out and rolled some joints in front of Vernon. "Ya'gona indulge with us.?" He asked him.

"Yeah, sure." he said. "Why not."

"We only partake fer medicinal reasons." Arlo said. "Ya'know it's good fer arthritis."

"You ain't got no arthritis." Vernon chuckled.

"Ya'see there—it works." Arlo answered seriously.

Wednesday morning early, Vernon hugged Mama and the boys. Told them he loved them and that he would return. All were crying when he got in his car and left.

The Tuesday night show had gone off without a hitch. Arlo again over-saw the action. Mama and Vernon had stayed in the kitchen for a little while before the band was to start. Mama asked Arlo where he learned the song he sang Saturday night.

"Oh, that little ol'song." he said. "I learnt it from Charles Darwins. You know—that evolutions guy what thought we came from apes."

Everyone glared at him. Vernon smiled.

"You know Maurine, I really like that boy." And they retired to bed.

That night everyone had a rip-roaring rowdy redneck good time and consumed a lot of beer. And the intellectual and philosophical erudite redneck culture, continued to live on at Mama's Place. Remember, when someone refers to you as a redneck. Be sure to thank them.

the end.

ABOUT THE AUTHOR

IN A NUTSHELL

Jim Feazell—Retired motion picture stunt actor, filmmaker and singer-songwriter. Jim worked in Hollywood for 22 years as a western stuntman and headed his own film production company for 15 years in El Dorado, Arkansas / Tucson, Arizona / and Hollywood, California. He has written numerous theatrical screenplays ie; Time And Time Again / Two Guns To Timberline / The Hurting / A Deadly Obsession / Wheeler / Psycho From Texas / etc. He was affiliated with AFTRA, SAG, MPAA, MPSA and WGA-West. Since retiring from motion picture production. Jim has become a novelist. This current book, "Mama's Place" will be his sixth to date. He writes mostly in the Supernatural and Mystery genre.